What I'd Give for Just . .

One More Anything

J BOYKIN BAKER

One More Anything

Published by True Promise Press

ISBN: 979-8-9864926-7-4 (hardcover)
ISBN: 979-8-9864926-8-1 (paperback)
ISBN: 979-8-9864926-9-8 (eBook)
ISBN: 979-8-218-17412-5 (audiobook)

Books are available in quantity for promotional or premium use. For information, email info@jboykinbaker.com or visit www.jboykinbaker.com.

To women everywhere who have experienced the kind of friendship that has enriched their lives through love, laughter, and yes, even tears.

All the Raves From Girlfriends Everywhere

I just finished *One More Anything,* and I absolutely loved it. This is a MUST-READ story of five ladies who share an amazing friendship of love and dedication. I laughed, cried, and was truly touched by their journey together. J Boykin Baker is a talented and gifted writer. I can't wait for her next book.

– Teddy L.

Women's devotion to each other is an absolute blessing from above. When cherished like a gift, the love shared is nothing less than extraordinary. *One More Anything* is an incredible testament to the power of friendship and is a great read.
   – Elizabeth T.

This book is one every woman will love. You will laugh hard and cry at times because it touches at the heart of what true friendships are all about. We love each other through the good times and the bad.
   – Becky W.

I just finished the book with much laughter and tears on my part. I especially like the ending. Let us all cherish every moment and remain cognizant of what we would give for one more anything with those whom we dearly love. Bravo Ms. Baker, for another excellent read.
— Donna H.

I loved, loved, loved this book! Do you really have friends who did all of this?
— Carey R.

I am loving this book, but my laughter and tears are causing concern for people sitting around me! LOL. I'm so grateful for the timing in reading this beautiful story. This is a winner!
— Maureen C.

Acknowledgments

To Patty Little, who made my writing readable.

To the incredible women in my life who gave me great writing material. You know who you are!

To Mary Ann Smith for the fabulous cover.

To Maggie McLaughlin for turning lots of paper into a polished book.

To my readers for being there to fine-tune every page.

To my husband, Ben, who now claims to be destitute, for financing my book-writing hobby.

Introduction

How many times had I made this trip? I wondered as that old familiar pain tugged, taking hold once again. I stopped the car, then carefully pulled into a small space. Hoping it was a legal parking spot, I maneuvered back and forth several times as I bounced and scraped tires on the curb. *Besides*, I thought, *this spot is as close as I can get to that damn bell tower.* Cutting off the engine of the tacky, bright blue car, I glanced down at my watch and slid back into the worn seat, trying to find room to stretch my legs. Due to my poor planning, this was the only rental car available when I arrived at the Atlanta airport. Shaking my head, I shrugged; it was idiotic not to call ahead to reserve a car for a Friday. But today's concern had drowned out any thoughts of a car. There were so many other issues to contemplate, to hopefully settle, and to possibly even forgive. *Oh well*, I thought. *We'll figure it out when I get there and confess. We just have to. Can I get in trouble for telling tales without permission?* I laughed to myself. *Jailhouse orange is not my best color.*

My plane had arrived on time that rainy morning, which put me in Atlanta nearly three hours before 'the meeting.' I looked at the muddy trail that wandered up to that foreboding tower. It was going to be a slippery trek to the top. It made me weary to even think about the climb. Looking again at my watch, I decided with no other place in particular to go, I might try to take a short nap before the others arrived.

I had hoped to sleep a little on the plane since Delta left Wilmington before six o'clock that morning. I had gotten up at three to ensure I had thirty minutes for a much-needed cup of coffee, maybe even two. Then after getting dressed, the hour's drive from Bald Head Island to the airport in Wilmington, especially in the dark, always seemed to put me in a tizzy. Would I remember that last turn, hit a deer, or have a flat tire? Plus, to be truthful, I'm not a morning person, but unfortunately, the woman seated beside me on the airplane loved mornings and would not shut up.

Trying to graciously listen as she explained the heartache of her mother's recent death, the irony of our conversation crossed my mind—this precious woman, whose grief was so apparent, was headed to Atlanta to plan her mother's funeral.

Cracking two car windows, I leaned back against the headrest and sighed. The rain had stopped, and the sun was appearing as sporadic yellow rays that seemed to be pushing the stubborn gray clouds out of their path. It was so pretty to look at. But as I closed my eyes, determined to fall asleep, vivid memories carried my mind back to happier times, to the beginning of the year my whole life changed. I opened my eyes and smiled as the tears fell. Had that morning actually been over twelve years ago? I leaned down and pulled out one of the gifts I had brought for each of my friends. I opened it up and began to read.

The Call

I had just arrived at the office when my assistant, Renee Hughes, met me at the front door of Jordan Designs, an interior design firm I had started four years ago. Thankfully, it had grown exponentially through hard work, good connections, and a lot of luck. But the pace was about to kill me.

"You've already had three calls this morning from the Brookhaven Hospital," Renee said. "They're adding some kind of a new building and want to set up an appointment as soon as possible. So I scheduled the meeting for this afternoon and moved your hair appointment to next week."

"What?" I put my hands on my forehead and huffed, "You've got to be kidding!" I lowered my head and exposed the two inches of gray roots in my dark brown hair. "Look at this. I look like a skunk. When next week?"

Renee turned and headed back to her office, mumbling, "Late Friday."

Pulling out my eyebrow pencil, I frowned and walked into the bathroom. There, I spent thirty minutes covering my gray roots before calling an office meeting. Our business was on overload, and I needed to see if any of the other designers had openings in their schedules before promising to tackle a new project at the hospital.

I asked Renee to gather everyone for a quick meeting to discuss projects in the works and their various timelines. Valerie, bless her heart, was always ready for anything. Raising her hand, she offered, "Jan, you'll be handling the difficult part of working with the client. The drawings can be completed by the CAD operators. I can pull finishes. Let's do it!"

I laughed and asked, "But do what?" I had no idea what the hospital had in mind. Yet, it was an excellent opportunity to get our foot in the door with this particular client.

After our meeting, I grabbed a bite of lunch: peaches, cottage cheese, and four stale crackers from a canister. Then, stopping by the fabric library, I motioned to Valerie. We picked up briefcases and left for a two o'clock meeting with a Ms. Moore at the hospital. She was the Vice President of Women's Services, and hopefully would explain the possible new project. Walking into the lobby, I had no idea just how important this meeting would turn out to be.

I Want Her!

Looking around at the surroundings, Valerie commented, "Jan, this whole place needs a redo. Look at the colors . . . pale pink and dusty blue? They might have been in vogue ten years ago, but, good grief, they're dated."

I laughed and agreed as we walked up to the circular, mahogany receptionist's desk and asked an older lady dressed in that awful pink color, "Liz Moore, please?"

"Down the long pink hallway to your right. Her suite is the first door on the left."

Entering the Women's Services Administrative Suite, I noted that the colors remained the same. Everything was clean and neat, but the hospital needed a serious facelift. Peering in several of the offices, the décor just got worse. The furnishings were a hodgepodge of different styles and wood tones. It certainly didn't present a very professional atmosphere. Quite frankly, the setting was unusually bad for a hospital in Atlanta; most big-city medical facilities had advanced to a more modern look a long time ago.

Taking a seat in two mismatched chairs that were staggered along the hallway, Valerie and I looked around for a receptionist's desk. Busy employees came and went, smiled, and said hello, but offered no help. After about fifteen minutes, I heard one of the most infectious laughs I could ever remember. It was coming from an office directly behind where we were sitting.

Why not? I thought as I stood and walked to the office belonging to the laugh.

Knocking on the doorframe, I watched as a rather imposing woman cupped her hand over her phone, laughed again, and asked with a contagious smile, "Do you need something?"

"I have an appointment with Liz Moore. Can you let her know that we're here?"

"Oh, my goodness! What time is it?" The woman looked at her watch, said a quick goodbye into the phone, and rushed over to extend her hand. "I'm Liz. You must be Jan. Excuse me, Ms. Jordan. Please come in and take a seat."

Flustered by Liz's huge personality, I took a seat. Then realized I had forgotten Valerie. I rushed back to the door, motioned for her to join me, and the two of us sat down in the faded blue velvet chairs in front of Liz's desk.

"My real name is Elizabeth, but everyone calls me Liz." She didn't take a breath. "You can, too," she laughed. Then she motioned out of her window. "If you go around back, you can see that we've already started on the addition. But we had a mutiny this morning, and two of our top surgeons threw a fit when they saw the plans for the interiors." Shaking her head, she continued, "Minutes later, our pediatric neurosurgeon came stomping into my office, tossed your card on my desk, and demanded, 'I want her.'"

She chuckled, "Evidently, you did his office. Now, just so you understand, we don't like changing horses midstream at this hospital. But he's our golden boy, so we have to take him seriously. You've got the job and I just need to know how soon you can start," Liz said, laughing again, as she waited for my answer.

Valerie looked at me and whispered, "Start on exactly what?"

I couldn't help but laugh myself. "It's not that simple, Liz. First, you need to tell me what we are starting on."

"On the PICU building," she said as she fumbled in her desk drawer. Pulling out a card, she added, "Here's the card of our architect. He'll tell you everything you need to know. And while you're doing the new addition, I'd like my office redone. I'm sick of these colors. Everyone here gets to do their office any way they like. I inherited all of this from my predecessor. Guess I'm ready for a new look. Something nice and fancy, but we can talk about all that later." She paused briefly, tilted her head, and added, "There's something else you should know. We've got a board meeting next Friday morning, and they will want to see what the inside of the new building is going to look like. I'm sure that won't be a problem." She smiled and added, "I've heard only good things about you ladies.

"Oh yes. Just so you know, we dress really tailored around here . . . our administrator believes it's much more professional. You both look a little frilly, which will scare him to death. Wear blazers or something calm. You know, just tone it down." She sighed as she raised her brow. "I might as well be honest. The men on our board are tough nuts to crack. There's not a woman in sight. These doctors and business moguls think they know everything. Just warning you. Oh, and several hate pink." She stood and walked around her desk to lead us to the door. "I'll see you next Friday at eight o'clock sharp. The boardroom is on the second floor."

Walking out of the suite, back down the pink hallway, and to the front doors, we didn't make a sound. Once outside, Valerie looked my way and asked, "Why didn't you say something? It's now Friday, and we won't be able to meet with the architect until Monday. Somehow we have to get a plan ready by next Friday."

All I could do was laugh and say, "Don't worry about a thing. We'll make it happen. But I do have three concerns. First, I don't think I own a single blazer. Second, I'd better not have to cancel another hair appointment." Then, looking up toward my forehead, I raised my eyes, "And third, what in the hell is a PICU?"

Valerie's eyes widened. "A PICU? You don't know? I have no clue."

By the time we got to the car, Valerie was Googling and reading aloud the description of a Pediatric Intensive Care Unit. I had wanted to decorate the interiors of hospitals for years. Still most of our medical design thus far consisted of private physicians and dental offices. This would be an incredible opportunity for Jordan Designs, but it would definitely entail a huge learning curve, and we surely couldn't afford a mistake on our first hospital job.

Looking over at Valerie, I hesitantly assured her once again. "I've got all weekend to research this. We'll be A-Okay."

Traffic was already heavy that Friday afternoon as we pulled back into the office parking lot just before five. Our building was small but worked well for a design firm. It held seven private offices with two designers and their workstations in each office and three large libraries with work tables and samples of anything needed to put a design project together. That included fabrics, flooring, tile, furniture catalogs, and more. In addition, there was a business office and a small reception area, a Computer Aided Design room with two CAD operators, and thankfully, with this many women, three bathrooms. The colors that flowed throughout were a crisp green and white with brick-red accents, and even a little golden yellow added here and there. It was a pleasant place to work and easy on the eyes. There were no bold patterns of any consequence to distract or compete with our design visions. Although I have to admit work was fun for me, and I loved a new challenge, today's meeting with Liz seemed like the most daunting task of my design career. I had no idea what she had just hired us to decorate.

However, God is good, and we truly witnessed a miracle that day. The minute Valerie and I walked in, Renee stepped out of her office and asked to speak with me. Feeling a little frantic, I asked, "Can it wait?"

"I think you'll want to hear what I've got to say," Renee said with a sparkle in her eyes.

I stopped, raised my hands, and said, "What?"

"A young woman is sitting in my office. She's a designer, recently moved to Atlanta, and is looking for a job."

I huffed and started to walk away. "Not now."

"Wait a minute," she said as she grabbed my arm. "Her specialty is hospital design. She's been the in-house designer for two hospitals in Charlotte for the last five years" She smiled, "Lots of experience."

I turned, walked toward my office, rolled my eyes, and said, "Please, by all means, send her back."

"Her name is Pat Farmer, and here's her resume." Renee handed me the folder she had been holding at her side.

After a lengthy conversation with Pat, I felt better about the pediatric project. Pat had worked in North Carolina on a similar pediatric intensive care unit at Memorial outside of Charlotte. She would be invaluable in understanding codes and unique requirements for this specialized building.

I raised my eyes toward heaven. I had always known how important prayer was in my life. But today, I witnessed a prayer for help being answered at lightning speed. Our new hire was starting her first project Monday morning.

Lollipops, Doll Furniture, and a Rhinestone Blazer

❧

Our first meeting with the architect went well that Monday morning. Even though David Russ was to head up the new pediatric project and was a little gruff, he seemed pleased with the Jordan design team. Valerie, Pat, and I assured him we'd be ready for the presentation on Friday.

The next three days had everyone, and I mean everyone, in the office helping in one way or another, and the presentation was actually ready by noon on Thursday. It had been a true miracle, and if I do say so myself, it looked amazing. We had used various shades and hues of primary colors, being careful to avoid blues and pinks. All was packed and ready to go.

Thursday evening, when I got home, I gave my husband, Matt, a quick kiss and rushed upstairs. He knew what was scheduled for the following day and was used to my panic attacks. Searching my closet, I found a solitary blazer. It was a linen-plaid mixture of various shades of purple. It was sort of subtle, even though it had a few rhinestones on the shoulders. Trying it on with a black top, skirt, and shoes, I added a short gold necklace, a few bracelets, and earrings. Studying my reflection in the mirror, I hoped the outfit would complement the primary colors of the presentation perfectly. Now, everything was ready, including me.

The alarm sounded at six-thirty that Friday morning. I figured Valerie and Pat were probably on their way to set up the boardroom for our presentation. I needed to hurry. Just then, my son, Greg, walked into the bedroom complaining that his tire was flat and he needed a ride to school. Matt had already left for an early-morning flight to Raleigh, so this task would fall on my shoulders. All I could think of was the prospect of Atlanta traffic and now, this added stop.

After dropping Greg off and breaking every speed limit, I breathed deeply and pulled into the hospital parking lot. It was seven fifty-four. I had six minutes to find the board room. Hurrying inside and squeezing into a packed elevator, I arrived on the second floor. Rushing to the end of the main hallway, I thankfully spotted the mahogany boardroom doors and Liz pacing as she looked at her watch.

When she spotted me, she turned with hands on

her hips and laughed that incredible laugh of hers. Then teasingly, she looked at her watch and whispered, "If you worked for me, I'd fire your ass! Let's go." She turned, looked back over her shoulder, and added, "Is that the only blazer you own?"

I didn't say a word. I just followed Liz into the boardroom. When we entered, I could hear the board members oohing and aahing over our colorful balloons that were tied to each chair as they picked up giant, swirled lollipops at each seat. There was doll-sized furniture strategically placed up and down the center of the conference table. Each piece was painted in a bold color represented in the presentation. Buckets of various candies in the same primary colors were placed between the furniture pieces. All of the decorations looked child-friendly. I walked to the front of the room and took my seat between Valerie and Pat.

Liz approached the podium at eight on the dot, welcomed the group, introduced our team, and turned the meeting over to me. I began by inviting the guests to open their suckers and think back to a time when they were little boys and how frightening a hospital could be. It was hard not to laugh as I watched some of Atlanta's most sophisticated men licking lollipops while others reached for pieces of candy from colorful buckets. Next, I explained our color choices and the artistic elements as they savored the sweets. The men seemed very interested, even though I was sure they'd never thought of a hospital having this much excitement and creativity on the walls, floors, windows, and furniture. Lordy, I hoped they liked it. This was our one shot to please.

After explaining the last areas, I reiterated how the colors would connect with little children's thoughts. For example, red could be described as cherry, a deep pink could be raspberry, yellows could be lemon, and the purples, which perfectly matched my blazer, could be called grape. The board members began to nod; they seemed to be on board.

I sat the last of the samples down and asked if they had any questions. One of the doctors asked, "Is that pink really necessary?"

I figured he was one of the doctors behind Liz's warning. "Why no, sir, that's not pink at all. It's now raspberry."

"Well," he grinned and added, "I guess I like raspberry, but not pink."

With that, everyone stood and walked over to shake hands. They complimented our vision, took their suckers, balloons, and handfuls of candy from the bright buckets, and headed out for their day.

Liz walked over in shock. "I would have never believed it. That group has never agreed on anything. But after you had them drowning in a sugar high, I honestly think you could have told them you were planning to paint the whole place black, and they would have said okay!" She shook her head as she initialed the bright and cheerful presentation boards. "Let's do this!"

Though neither of us realized a thing that day, a bond was birthed. A bond between Liz and myself. A beautiful and treasured bond for a lifetime.

Competitive Edge?

It was amazing how quickly my friendship with Liz developed as we worked side by side on the new building. The job had now expanded into bringing various softer and deeper shades of the new colors into the entire hospital, along with a standards package that outlined the coordination of office furnishings. So finally, the hospital was being given that much-needed new look. As Jordan Designs' responsibilities grew and time passed, it seemed as if Liz and I spent more time together than we did with our individual families. Both of us worked tirelessly on the PICU, but the long hours didn't seem like work at all. We were having too much fun getting to know each other and the ins and outs of each of our lives.

We'd talk about my daughter, Alice, who was attending her senior year at Salem College in North Carolina and loving every minute of her independence, and my son, Greg. He was a junior in high school and played nearly every sport offered, alongside his peaked interest in girls. My husband, Matt, was always a topic of discussion. He was an executive with a large corporation and traveled extensively. With our insane schedules, I was grateful for a housekeeper who could come early or stay late. I was juggling lots of balls, but life was good, and my new friend seemed to understand it all, as her life was much the same.

Liz had twin girls who were seven years younger than Alice. The two had just entered a private high school in Virginia, and she and her husband were now enjoying quality time as empty nesters. Or so I thought. But I could tell every now and then, by Liz's expressions when her husband was mentioned, that there might be some strains in that relationship, as she had more irons in the fire than anyone I had ever known. Her job was intense; she was a gourmet cook and served on several nonprofit boards in a hands-on capacity. On top of all that, her sense of humor made Liz hilarious to be around, and she was in demand as a speaker. She loved telling jokes, especially if they were a little off-color, and would laugh that contagious cackle. Yet, I came to know a deeper, more compassionate side of this new friend. Her generosity and devotion to all she loved came first. I had heard of people who were 'larger than life,' but she was the first person I could remember who epitomized that description.

Liz's husband, Bill, was an attorney, and over several of our evenings out as couples, he and Matt had become friends, or better said, as friendly as most men can manage. On one of these evenings, Liz seemed preoccupied. After a little, I asked if she was okay. Without a smile, she looked into my eyes and said, "I have a concern about others in the hospital and their perception of our friendship."

"What? I don't understand." I couldn't imagine what she meant.

"Jan, technically speaking, you are a vendor, and I fear our friendship could raise eyebrows with the hospital's ethics committee. Vendors are to be kept at arm's length so as not to give the impression of favoritism."

"Oh, Liz, I would never want either of us to be questioned regarding ethics." I asked, "What should we do?" She never answered as she was caught up in our husbands' conversation.

But, the next afternoon, Liz called a meeting with the CEO and Chairman of the hospital board to discuss her hesitancy concerning our friendship. She was quickly told they would not be opposed if this friendship kept me working there rather than for the competition. In their words, "Jordan Designs was their competitive edge, and Liz was, by all means, to keep me from working down the street for another hospital."

Now, with that green light, we actually became more like sisters. We'd take walks and share personal issues, concerns about our children, and an occasional business situation. Things blossomed into a comfortable relationship, mainly because we had so much in common. I got a call from Liz one Saturday morning. "Jan, I've got the whole day free. What's your schedule?"

"I'm at Greg's baseball game, but I should be home by eleven at the latest," I replied.

"Why don't I pick you up at noon? I'd love your company on a long walk, and then we should go get our nails done. I'll make that appointment for three o'clock."

"Sounds great! We'll have time to grab a bite to eat between the walk and our nails."

"Perfect. See you at noon." Liz clicked off.

Greg had one of his best games ever. He hit two home runs and pitched an impressive no-hitter. After all of the congratulations on the win, Matt and I left for home. I changed into cooler clothes for the walk, fixed Matt a BLT sandwich, and grabbed a tube of lipstick when I heard Liz's horn blaring. Looking in the mirror, I put the color on my lips and blotted as I rushed out.

Liz suggested trying a different walking path simply for the variety; it was a heavily wooded path. As we set off, my designing mind kicked into gear. I should say overdrive. "Oh, Liz! Wouldn't this be the ideal place for a quaint little cottage? You know, one with shutters that have heart cut-outs? Can't you just see Snow White running around playing with the seven dwarfs? And deer jumping as fluffy little rabbits play in the grass? And colorful flowers popping up everywhere?"

Liz shook her head as she said, "You can really see all that, can't you?"

I admitted that I could see every bit of it. I could even hear the little birds singing.

"Jan, you know that most people don't think like you. I could never see that in a million years. But we might want to take some of your ideas and do something clever for a children's garden at the hospital." Then, she fussed. "But we're not going to think about work today."

Just then, I heard a splat and noticed a bird had taken aim on Liz's shoulder. We both started laughing as she said, "Can you believe this? And I tried my best to look cute today! Thank heavens I wore a jacket." Pulling it off, she tied the unsoiled section around her waist as we continued walking, and she said, "We'll leave the birds out of the children's garden."

An hour later, we got back in her car and decided to skip lunch. Taking several sips of water and deep breaths, we headed for the salon.

Talking non-stop as we pulled into the strip mall, we didn't realize that she had cut off the car beside us from also pulling in. The driver clearly didn't appreciate her driving as evidenced by his blaring horn. Though we politely waved, we had business to take care of and hurriedly parked, noting that we had less than five minutes to get to the appointment.

The offended driver also parked and walked straight toward our car. It was easy to see that he was not happy. With a stern voice, he said, "You two need driving lessons! You do realize you cut me off? I had to circle around to make my turn."

Liz just rolled her eyes. "I would love to stay here and chat with you about this, but we have an appointment to get our nails done. They don't like for anyone to be late." With that, she took my hand and pulled me toward the salon door. I looked back and watched the poor man throw his hands up and walk away.

Entering the salon, I realized we were the only two in the entire shop who spoke English, as Vietnamese seemed to be the preferred tongue. Liz was a regular client at this salon, however, and she had worked out a method of communication with a few simple words. Unfortunately, I was unable to follow her example, and my frustration was building. It reached a tipping point when I tried to explain exactly how I wanted my nails filed. I grabbed the Emory board and began demonstrating; I wanted my nails curved, not blunt. My example apparently wasn't helpful as the technician paid no attention, and now both our tempers were on edge by the end of my manicure. I could hear Liz laughing every now and then as our eyes met in the wall of mirrors. I tried to smile, but it was a horrible appointment.

When we each stepped to the counter to pay, Liz patted the owner's hand and said, "Don't worry. I promise never to bring her back."

Leaving, we walked next door to A Touch of Class for a much-needed glass of wine as we laughed over the bird poop, the furious driver, and the difficulty of a language barrier.

Late one evening in early April, Liz called and explained that she and four other close friends were going to a lake house for the weekend. It belonged to one of the other ladies; her name was Dorothy. But Fran, another group member, had to drop out of the trip to care for an aging parent. That left space for me if I would like to join them. Liz explained that Dorothy was a pastor's wife. She and her husband, Frank, led a large Baptist church in Conyers, and their lake house was at Lake Oconee near Augusta. From Liz's description, it was very nice, and there was plenty of room if I didn't mind sharing a bedroom. She explained that the group enjoyed the serenity of the lake but spent most of their time shopping in nearby historical areas. Continuing, she described the others who would be going.

There would be Katherine, the CFO of a prestigious accounting firm in the heart of Atlanta, and she was pregnant. Sue, Dorothy's co-worker from an earlier time, would also be coming, and she was with a headhunting firm called Medical Personnel, Inc. The ladies had planned to bring wine and lots of snack foods, and we'd have lunch on our shopping trips. The shopping sounded like a perfect weekend, and I was certainly up for that activity.

I checked with Matt, and our weekend was open. He would be home to attend all of Greg's sporting events, so I was free to go. Liz would pick me up at five on Friday at my office.

Have You Ever Seen "Deliverance"?

Friday turned out to be absolutely gorgeous, with a high of seventy. It was spring, and the dogwoods, azaleas, and daffodils lined the highway. They were in full bloom, and the colors were spectacular as Liz and I drove toward the lake. Typically a nightmare, traffic leaving Atlanta actually wasn't too bad. The two of us pulled into Dorothy's driveway just after six-thirty. The lake house wasn't like I had expected at all. Thinking of lake houses from my childhood, they were always rustic, but this was a lovely white cottage with a manicured lawn and steps that meandered down to a boat dock on the lake. Casually rocking back and forth, a silver pontoon boat was moored at the pier.

Walking inside, Liz and I were loaded down with luggage, purses, and bags of groceries. But, as a designer, I stopped to look around. The traditional interior was lovely and had three bedrooms. Dorothy and Sue shared one, Liz and I took the twin beds in a second room, and Katherine took the smaller room with a fancy, little day bed.

After lengthy introductions, we opened a bottle of wine and decided to walk down to the dock. Having decided a sunset cruise on the pontoon boat would be relaxing, we laughed, watching as everyone gingerly climbed aboard. All but Liz and I had changed out of work clothes before arriving, and they were now comfortable in sweats or jeans. But having been picked up from the office, Liz and I were still dressed in expensive outfits and good jewelry. As we talked, my comments seemed awkward, and to be honest, I felt like an outsider. These women had been friends for a long time.

The group chatted about shared memories of which I had no knowledge. Katherine seemed polite and appeared to be nearly ready to deliver. She was blonde, blue-eyed, and a classic beauty who seemed slightly reserved as she sipped from her water bottle and occasionally rubbed her tummy.

Dorothy was extremely warm and welcoming but kept apologizing for several areas in the house with spotty decorating. She was also blonde and attractive, with skin like a porcelain doll. Not someone I imagined who would have been a close friend with the boisterous Liz. But first impressions are not always correct. Dorothy was relatively quiet and had a soft laugh in contrast to Liz's uninhibited, robust ways. But I could tell they thoroughly enjoyed each other.

At first, I thought Sue might be Native American with her dark hair and olive complexion. She had a very kind way about her, but at times seemed distant, even sad. I later learned that Sue had been married only to have lost her husband in an automobile accident. That was ten years ago, and she had never remarried. The love of her life now was her dog, Lilly. I understood Lilly was highly spoiled and treated more like a child than a pet. If I wanted to be friends with Sue, I would have to love Lilly. Thankfully, a rule of no-pets had been put into place for any of their trips, which meant I would have to wait to meet this member of the group at a later time. But there was no doubt in my mind that this puppy had taken Sue's heart hostage.

It was interesting that they all had such high-powered careers and, yet, such diverse lives. Katherine, for instance, was much younger, and they called her 'the mascot.' She and Dorothy became good friends when her firm took over the financials of Dorothy's church.

I also learned that these women had been making the lake house trips for several years and had become quite a congenial group. Listening to the conversations as we cruised the lake, I could tell that I was going to like these ladies. Together we all could appreciate the weekend's respite from the pressures and commitments of busy lives.

After a successful Saturday shopping trip to a lovely Victorian mansion in Madison, Georgia, it was time for another short cruise before we went to dinner at a nearby pub. Liz got the wine, I found some plastic glasses, and Dorothy brought a loaf of French bread and various types of cheese to the boat. As we laughed at Liz's latest joke and slowly puttered out to the lake's center, the silver boat jerked and stopped. Unconcerned, Dorothy shrugged her shoulders and calmly said, "That's unusual."

Liz quickly asked, "Well, just how do we get it going again?"

Dorothy walked over and played with a button, to no avail. She turned to Liz and said, "I don't know. This has never happened before."

I looked over at Katherine. "You okay?" I had noticed her moving around, seeming to try for a more comfortable position.

"I'm fine. That pain must have just been gas . . . or the baby's head is under my ribcage."

Just then, a rickety, old boat could be seen in the distance. We waved and yelled for help as it came closer. Soon, the power boat pulled up alongside ours. It was apparent that all four men had enjoyed more than a few drinks. But Dorothy explained that the pontoon boat had simply stopped, and we needed to be pulled ashore.

I was a little nervous, as the men were flirty and obviously 'country bumpkins,' but when they saw Katherine's belly, they quieted down. I decided to trust Liz and Dorothy to handle the situation and just sat quietly. The scruffy men proved to be innocent but a wee bit selfish. They weren't interested in our boat problems; they had merely pulled up to ask if we had any extra beer! Once they found out there was none available, they turned and sped off, yelling that they would try to send help. *Sure*, I thought. *They'll have trouble finding their way home, much less their way back to us.*

We sat there for another hour, but help never came. The sun had begun to set, and the sky and water were growing darker. But while sitting on the perfectly still boat discussing our options and Katherine's bladder needs, we suddenly caught a glimpse of the shoreline. We had actually drifted nearer to land. Liz jumped up and said, "We can pull it! Two of us can jump in and pull the front dock lines. The rest of you can paddle." The scary part was that her suggestion seemed to make absolute sense in our befuddled state of mind.

We had dressed up earlier to go shopping and hadn't bothered changing. I looked around. None of us were wearing anything remotely close to a swimsuit. But that didn't stop Liz. She pulled off her slacks

27

and said, "I spent two hundred dollars on these pants, and I'm not about to get them wet in this lake."

Dorothy didn't say a word; she just jumped into the water, clothes and all. Liz finished throwing the lines out to Dorothy as she paddled back, grabbed them, and was ready to pull the boat. Then, standing in her underwear, Liz yelled, "Dorothy, is it cold?"

"No! It's great!" Dorothy called, "Jump in!"

With that assurance, Liz jumped. The minute her body hit the water, she screamed, "Liar! It's freezing!"

Dorothy laughed as she tried to keep her head above water and promised, "Pulling this boat will warm you up." She looked back at Sue and me and said, "Now, lay down on your stomach along the front and start paddling with your arms as hard as possible. Katherine, you just sit there and pray."

After struggling for about ten minutes, Liz and Dorothy realized that as they pulled harder and harder, we were paddling against them in the wrong direction. Yelling in unison, they ordered, "Go to the back of the boat, lay down, and paddle in the opposite direction. With that minor correction, we slowly drew closer to the shore. When we reached a shallow area where Dorothy and Liz could touch the bottom, they began pulling the boat faster as they walked toward the end of an old, dilapidated dock. Both ladies, soaked and freezing, one in white panties, climbed up the ladder and tied the boat to the cleats on the leaning dock. Only then did they remember Liz was half naked. Sue looked around and found two cushion covers. Throwing both to Liz, she wrapped and tied them around her bottom with an extra rope. Sue leaned over to the ladder and threw Liz's pants and a towel onto the dock. Remaining dressed in the cushion covers, Liz grabbed the towel and helped Dorothy dry off. Realizing how ridiculous we all must have looked, everyone had to laugh. Our outfits ran the spectrum from a burlesque show to a board meeting. I thought, *thank the Lord for humor.*

By then, the night was pitch black. We had no flashlight or boat lights, but I noticed a light flickering in the distance. My immediate concern became exiting the boat to escape any danger. Sue climbed up the ladder and onto the dock. Next, we had to get Katherine on the ladder. I gently pushed while Sue pulled. Dorothy and Liz were still trying to catch their breath. In minutes, Katherine was safe and standing on the dock. Next, I blindly maneuvered to steady the rails on the ladder as I climbed up. Liz laughing at my efforts, hollered, "For God's sake, don't fall. You'll sink like a rock with all that jewelry you've got on!"

Everyone laughed, including Katherine, as she managed to keep her balance and exit the dock onto dry, steady land. I looked up, the light I had seen earlier seemed closer, and my thoughts went straight to the movie, *Deliverance.* Sure enough, two men approached. Both were carrying shotguns.

Hiding behind one of the men, a little girl stared at

us in silence. I breathed a sigh as I thought, *surely, they won't shoot us in front of an innocent child*. Then something strange happened. The child stepped in front of the light. As I looked closer at the beautiful little girl, her hair was different from any hair I had ever laid eyes on. It looked like a stiff, scratchy Brillo pad, and I had never wanted to touch anything that badly. I was dying to see if it was real and if it moved.

One of the men spoke and asked what we were doing on his land. No one answered, probably due to the guns and that hair. No one said a thing. Then a dog barked. Shaken out of our stupor, all five of us tried to nervously explain the situation.

"Hold it! Hold it! Hold it!" he exclaimed. "One at a time."

Dorothy's voice trembled, "Our boat stopped and wouldn't restart. So we swam and dragged it over here. We need to use your telephone . . . if we can. Please?"

"We don't have a phone. And how would I know what your intentions are if we did?"

Liz, still half-naked, took over the conversation. "Listen, if we had any ulterior motives," she pointed to Katherine's obviously pregnant belly and continued, "we wouldn't have brought her. We need to get her home, and it's on the other side of the lake."

"Me and my son can take you. That is if you don't mind riding in a flatbed truck," he growled.

Each of us waited for someone else to speak up.

Finally, Katherine looked at us and asked, "Has anybody got a better idea?" She turned toward the older gentleman, the gun still at his side, and said, "Sir, we'd appreciate a ride home in your truck."

Looking at her belly, he answered, "You can ride up front with me and my granddaughter. My son will watch those ladies in the back."

By now, flickering stars filled the night sky as we helped one another onto the back of the flatbed. The son jumped on and pulled Liz on as she held tightly to her two-hundred-dollar pants in one hand, and the cushion covers hiding her wet panties in the other. Katherine managed to get into the cab seat. As she sat there waiting for us to get on board, she realized the driver was drunk as he said, "You remind me of my first wife . . . and I still love my first wife." She slid closer to the door and began to pray.

The wind picked up as the truck sputtered, jerked, and crossed the median several times. The night air was freezing. But only Liz complained as she said, "You should try this ride half naked!"

Finally, after nearly thirty minutes of cold and what had to be close to frostbite, the truck drove into Dorothy's welcoming drive. Never had we been so thankful to see the familiar site. Everyone scampered from the truck as the older man walked over to help Katherine, his granddaughter following close behind. When Katherine had her footing, he walked over to close the truck door, leaving his granddaughter unprotected.

My curiosity could wait no longer. I walked closer to the little girl and patted her head. "You're the cutest little thing!" I said as I smiled at the grandfather. Then I turned and rushed to follow my friends into the house.

When I walked inside, the ladies were in hysterics. Liz asked, "Okay, how'd it feel?"

I shrugged my shoulders and shuttered as I whispered, "It felt just as weird as it looked. Like a stiff Brillo pad with curls."

Needless to say, that was our last boat ride that weekend. But somehow, I wasn't an outsider anymore. I had passed my unspoken initiation by putting my hand on that sweet little head and describing the strangest hair ever. I was now a significant part of a memory.

On Tuesday of the following week, we realized how close we had come to a catastrophe. Katherine delivered a precious little boy.

Fire! Where's My Son?

Two weeks later, on a stormy summer afternoon, the unthinkable happened. I got a phone call at my office telling me that my house was on fire. It had been struck by lightning. All I could think of was my son. I panicked, wondering if he was okay. His part-time job for the summer was to clean out and paint all of our gutters. When I pulled out of the driveway that morning, he had been standing on a metal ladder leaning against metal gutters. I had blown him a kiss and waved goodbye. All I could imagine now was how lightning reacted to metal. I freaked knowing that a teenager doesn't have enough sense to get out of the rain. A mother knows these things. A hundred worried thoughts raced through my mind, going in a hundred different directions as I grabbed my keys and ran for my car.

Black smoke was evident as soon as I entered our

neighborhood. Then I saw our house. Flames shot through the roof of the one-story section that now had no walls. It was the exact area where my son had been painting that morning. My entire body went numb as tears exploded. *Where is he? How is he?*

There were firetrucks everywhere, and large hoses were pulled through the front door pouring gallons of water inside. And then I saw a blonde head. Being six foot, four inches, Greg was easy to spot, and he had never looked so gorgeous to his mama. I was beyond thankful. I pulled the car over to the curb, got out, and ran to him as quickly as I could. Holding him in my arms, I cried, "Are you okay? Are you okay?" as I checked every inch of his body.

It was like he reverted back to being a little boy. "I promise, Mom. I didn't do it. It was lightning!"

I nodded. "I was so afraid you were still on that ladder. I was terrified that lightning had struck you too."

"Mom, right before it happened, I had run out of sandpaper and went to buy more. I heard the boom when it hit. I had just come out of the hardware store."

After I'd checked to make sure Greg was unharmed, I ran over to one of the firefighters. I introduced myself before asking, "Is the fire out?"

"Almost, ma'am. We saved most of the two-story part of your home, but the one-story area is where the lightning discharged. We're still working on those blazes."

I thanked him profusely and then turned to greet caring and curious neighbors coming to check on us. From that point in time, most everything seemed to blur. My beautiful home, my nest for our family, was a wet, black mess. Smoke, soot, ashes, water, and the worst smell ever took over my senses.

Just then, Matt drove up, and I'll never forget the look on his face. He ran up and asked where Greg was. I pointed to a distraught young man sitting on the brick wall with his face in his hands. I could see the decision-making going on in Matt's eyes. Who needed his comfort more right now? Me or his son?

Later that afternoon, the fires were totally out, and some of the smoke began to disappear. There were no more flames in sight, but we had a new problem. Television reporters had descended, and they were giving out the address of our fire on the nightly news. Soon there was a steady stream of gawkers driving by and staring at our tragedy.

One thoughtful neighbor had brought lawn chairs for us to sit in as we had been pacing in the driveway. Matt and I gratefully sat down, mainly in silence, when I voiced the craziest thought. My whole life was in shambles, and I exclaimed, "What are we going to do for pots and pans?"

Matt looked at me as if I had lost my mind. "Jan! The ones we had were full of cobwebs! Why would you think of that?" He shook his head and added, "You haven't cooked in years!"

"I don't know. It seemed important . . . I just can't think."

Finally, the last fireman exited the front door. He and one of his team members placed yellow tape across the doorway. The fire chief then came over to talk to us. "We prefer that you wait to enter your home until you've contacted your insurance agent. Ask for an adjuster to meet you here in the morning. The two-story part of your home is pretty much intact. There's water and smoke damage, but you have a lot of valuable assets that need to be protected. With your address being given out on the news, there will likely be looters. We suggest you hire some form of security to guard the premises until your house can be secured."

"Looters? Security? Please tell me this is a bad dream." And then I asked another stupid question, "Don't you all have some fans that can get the smoke out tonight?"

He gave me a pitiful look and replied, "Ma'am, fans can't help this. Your house got so hot inside that your pantry is full of popped popcorn."

With that, the tears came again - and lasted for about three months.

When the adjuster came, he brought in a company that takes everything out of the home, cleans it, refinishes it, and does everything possible to return it to its original condition. Unfortunately, if there's fabric involved, it's a lost cause. The crew began to take fabric items to a dumpster that now sat in the middle of my front yard. The insurance adjuster stopped them and told them to spread it all out on the lawns. "We'll get pictures first. They have replacement insurance," he said.

I watched as they brought out everything from Greg's closet, Matt's closet, and finally, mine. Thank heavens, Alice was married. Everything important to her was in her new home in Winston-Salem. But, my bras and panties were scattered all over the front yard. Several folks stopped to ask if we were having a yard sale. Now, I had no front door and my red brick house was primarily black. That question made me want to fight. *A yard sale!*

That afternoon a clothes consultant came to put evaluations on our wardrobes. Matt started laughing as she asked questions about the articles. He pointed to Greg's things and said, "Don't worry about that pile. It looked as bad before the fire as it does now." Then he pointed to all the items from his own closet and said, "Put me down for a couple of suits, a blazer, some pants, and shirts, and I'll be good." And then he pointed to three-fourths of the yard covered with my belongings. He laughed, "Here's your problem!"

She picked up several of my items and agreed. "I'm going to need some help. Who wears all this stuff?"

That night we went to Marshall's and bought some

clothes that were nice enough to wear to do serious shopping at the mall. Our neighbors were so kind, and brought us breakfast, lunch, and dinner, along with every hygiene product we might need at the motel to which we had moved. We just kept working on the replacement list, all the while wondering if there was an end in sight. Matt looked at me and promised to leave me on the spot if I ever bought that much mess again.

Weeks passed as the reconstruction began, and our house seemed to be coming back to life while we made do in a small apartment near a railroad track. The worst sound in the world is a two a.m. train. But, thankfully, it was still more comfortable than a motel room. Yet, there was one constant during all of this confusion, devastation, and uncertainty. My four new friends, Liz, Dorothy, Katherine, and Sue, never left my side as they made sure to meet our needs.

There were daily phone calls, baskets of fruits and candies, flowers, and anything they could think of to cheer me up sent regularly. I would see Liz while I worked on the new PICU and other office areas. When she could tell I was having a rough day with contractors or our insurance company, she would have the four plan a lunch or dinner somewhere fun, and we'd all get together. Sometimes it was just *Five Guys* for a hamburger or one of them just dropping off a meal. But they would laugh with me when I wanted to cry. Or they'd cry with me when I tried and failed to laugh.

I had never known such friendships and thanked God daily for these extraordinary women. Through all of this, Matt had come to love and appreciate them and their husbands as much as I did. I learned that tragedy can take an unexpected turn in the twinkling of an eye. After one relaxing weekend at a lake house, I had experienced such a blessing, or better yet, four. These ladies had entered my life at just the right moment in time.

Christmas Aprons and Santa Hats

~~~

Before I knew it, it was time for Christmas festivities. Having literally just moved back into our house, decorating for Christmas hadn't even crossed my mind. After leaving work one night following an exhausting day, I stopped short as I pulled into our driveway. There was a wreath on the front door and candles in every window. The mailbox even held pine greenery and a huge red bow. Then I noticed a van pulled just behind the house as I drove past it and into the garage.

Quickly walking inside, I couldn't believe my eyes. There were two tall Christmas trees in the Great Room, completely decorated with my children's handmade ornaments that had been rescued from all of the soot. Stockings were hung, and the mantel displayed many of our cleaned and restored decorations. And those four precious friends were busy finishing their decorating. They were wearing

Christmas aprons and Santa hats and Liz was carrying a tray of wine glasses and Christmas cookies to the kitchen table. They even had cinnamon sticks and cloves simmering in a pot on the stove, and the fragrance was drifting throughout the house, completing the Christmas spirit in every room. Joining them for a glass of wine, we laughed, cried, and began our Christmas together.

With my house looking so festive, I decided to have a dinner party to thank my four new best friends and their husbands. Sue offered to bring dessert, Katherine was to supply the wine, Dorothy wanted to try a new recipe for a Christmas ham, and Liz planned to bring her special hors d'oeuvre of assorted crackers, cheeses, and jellies passed down from her grand-mother as a Christmas tradition. I was cooking fresh string beans sprinkled with almonds, a corn soufflé, and a congealed salad with carrots and pineapple. Then, as an afterthought, I remembered a recipe for homemade yeast rolls. They would be perfect for rounding out our dinner.

When the day came, I cooked the corn and beans and made the salad, and then I combined all the ingre-dients for the yeast rolls. As instructed, I covered the dough with a moist towel to allow it to rise. Then, hurrying to prepare the table with my Christmas china, silver, and crystal, I decided my centerpiece needed a little fluffing. Two hours later, I finished that task, and it was time to run upstairs and get dressed.

When I returned to the kitchen an hour later, I screamed, "No!" Yeast had done its job, and the volume of my rolls had expanded past the bowl onto the marble top of the island, down the side, and puddled on the floor.

Now, I have faced similar situations before and had the textbook solution. "Matt, it's me, sweetheart. On your way home, stop by Henri's and pick up two dozen yeast rolls. I really was going to make them homemade, but I simply don't have time." He laughed, asked me what I had burned, and promised to pick up the rolls. An hour later, as the doorbell rang, I had just gotten the last bit of the dough into the garbage disposal. I was sweating, but my secret was safe.

That night was quite a celebration as they raved over my yeast rolls while we planned our next trip. This time we would travel to New York and stay in my husband's company apartment off Fifth Avenue.

New York, New York

The five of us were to be in New York over the first weekend of February. We had purchased tickets for *Cats* on Broadway, reservations at the Four Seasons for dinner on Saturday night, and The Plaza for brunch on Sunday. All other time was reserved for serious wardrobe shopping. We had been concerned that Katherine might not be able to go. But she assured us she was comfortable leaving the baby with her husband, Keith, and a nanny. We reserved a car and driver, as none of us felt safe driving in New York, and there was a taxi strike at the time as well. Due to Atlanta traffic, we arrived at the airport in just the nick of time to get to our gate and boarded the flight. We had used frequent flyer miles to get the tickets upgraded to first class. In retrospect, that probably wasn't the best idea, as we all enjoyed several glasses of wine. One way or another, it had been a stressful week for all of us.

Arriving at LaGuardia, we located our driver and headed for the apartment. We had forgotten how cold February could be in New York City, and while we all had jackets, they were for the South and not nearly heavy enough. So our first order of business was to buy warmer coats.

After dropping off our luggage with the doorman, we asked the driver to take us to the garment district. None of us had ever been to the 'district' before. Men were rushing everywhere, pushing large racks of clothing. And they were so rude! No one bothered to utter 'excuse me' if they bumped into you or ran over your foot. It seemed we were invisible; they were busy, and we were in the way. We finally spotted a store-front nestled between the warehouses and walked into a fabulous world of furs. There was fox, mink, rabbit, squirrel, and any kind of fur we could imagine. We started looking through the racks.

Liz poked my side and said, "Pinch me. Is this heaven?"

When you're freezing, money takes a back seat to warmth. Before we knew it, I had settled for a black suede coat trimmed in silver fox. Dorothy found a mink jacket that fit her perfectly, Liz twirled around in a leopard cape that was striking with her auburn hair, and Katherine went for a full-length mink coat that was practically free compared to the ones we had seen in Atlanta. She rationalized that she was due a baby gift from her husband, and we all agreed. Sue found a unique black leather and mink vest with sleeves that could be added to make a jacket. We left that store broke but no longer feeling the cold, as most of our shopping money was now on our backs. The reality of what we had just done set in, and we agreed that the rest of our shopping that day would take place in the knock-off booths on Canal Street. That night we all went to the play in our fine new coats, carrying three-dollar Chanel clutches.

Katherine was prone to migraines and had limited her wine intake at dinner. But, the wine from the flight evidently hung around. She woke up Saturday morning in excruciating pain, but we weren't overly concerned. Katherine had a syringe with Imitrex in her carry-on bag, which normally addressed the problem. With her nursing background, Liz found it and was ready to inject, but she saw too late that it was a spring-loaded syringe. When she lifted it up, the spring released and shot the medication straight into the ceiling. Liz screamed, Katherine fell back on the bed, and the rest of us came running into the room. Liz put on her black pants under her nightgown, threw her new cape over her shoulders, and ran out the apartment's front door, shouting into her cell. No one had a clue what she was up to, including Katherine, and we were worried.

I asked, "What's she doing?"

Dorothy answered, "You don't ask. You just get out of her way."

Forty-five minutes later, Liz flew back into the room, opened a box with a new syringe, and injected Katherine. We prayed it was Imitrex, but where did she get it? Within a few minutes, Katherine was feeling some relief. With her quick thinking, Liz had called a doctor in Atlanta, who called the pharmacy closest to the apartment, and she had run three blocks, picked up the new syringe, and ran back. The thought of that leopard cape flowing behind her was hysterical but fitting. Honestly, she really was a superwoman.

By lunchtime, we were out shopping again. Feeling so dressed up in our furs, we headed for Bloomingdale's. It takes more than a migraine and a credit limit to curtail shopping in New York. Now if you've never been to Bloomingdale's in the heart of New York when they're having a sale, I'd like to recommend it. Loaded down with new shoes at reduced prices, perfumes for half the usual cost, and nightgowns to die for, we called the day a success.

As we were leaving, a salesperson tapped me on the shoulder. She explained that there were protestors from PETA outside the store, and they were throwing paint on anyone wearing fur. She handed us shopping bags to hide our coats inside, and we mashed them down firmly to make sure no fur was in sight. We may have successfully hidden the evidence, but we nearly froze to death while walking back to the apartment.

The only other issue we faced that day was communication. New York is multicultural, to say the least, but no one speaks Southern. Much less understand, "You-who!" when you're trying to get their attention.

After thawing out, dinner at the Four Seasons that night was superb. However, we were exhausted and decided to retire early to just talk. I learned so much more about these women that night. Liz opened up about her family issues and explained that her brother had been sick for years. She sobbed as she shared the battles the two had fought together, the medical treatments tried, and the sadness of not finding any answers. Eventually, he had passed away, and in her own way, Liz was still recovering. Katherine also struggled and shared the sadness of her mother's bouts with depression. Katherine loved her dearly, but could not break through her shell to cross the hurtful distance. When Dorothy opened up, she explained how difficult it was to live up to the expectations of a preacher's wife and was thankful people could not read her thoughts. Sue admitted that she lived in fear of being alone again should she ever lose Lilly. That night we shared our souls.

I had even revealed mine, something I had never done before with anyone besides Matt. My parents divorced when I was in my early thirties. I learned it didn't matter whether one was young or old; divorce was hurtful to a child. Unfortunately, the children are led to believe they must take a side, and when they make a choice or any decision, it usually ends up hurting someone. Sometimes everyone. I had promised myself years ago that I would never put my children through that pain, and I was thankful that Matt felt the same, even during our rough patches.

By the way, *Cats* was amazing, and we had hummed *Memories* for the next three months.

What? You've Got to Be Kidding!

Having been back home from New York for nearly a month, I got a call from Dorothy. Sue had had a stroke. She was only forty-seven years old; this couldn't possibly be happening. She was too young. I cleared my schedule for the day and headed to St. Michael's Hospital. When I got there, Liz and Dorothy were in the waiting room. They hadn't been able to reach Katherine as she was out of town on business. Finally, a nurse entered the waiting room and filled us in on Sue's situation. She was very fortunate, and the stroke had not left any permanent damage that was identifiable at this point. However, she would be in intensive care for several days, and visitors would be limited to family members alone. The waiting room was so quiet that day; I could hear myself thinking. We were all worrying about the same things. *Who's looking after Lilly? And how can we identify as family?*

The four of us took turns checking on Lilly as we awaited updates from the family on Sue's condition. Thankfully, we found a well-recommended dog sitter who was able to move into Sue's house and spoil Lilly around the clock. Katherine called the minute she got back in town to see what she could do. We all felt so helpless, but Sue had a supportive family, and now, an anal dog sitter, and the four of us. We even supplied gourmet dog food to ensure Lilly ate better than our own families.

One afternoon, while Sue was still at the hospital, the four of us met at her house to spruce it up for her homecoming. I had some accessories and florals at the office that I felt would work nicely for a little fresh decorating. That afternoon, I went back to Sue's to hang a few pictures, arrange the accessories, and place a plant or two to bring a little of the outside in. Unfortunately, a bee as well, but my shoe took care of him.

By now, Sue was looking great, but she was so pretty anyway. One would have never guessed she had been through such a medical ordeal. Her only orders involved a daily blood thinner for the rest of her life. Two days later, our patient was home with her beloved Lilly and the new dog sitter. Within another week, Sue was back to caring full-time for Lilly, and we were promised for her own self as well.

The Silver Trip

As soon as we were confident that Sue was truly behaving and feeling stronger, we decided to go to Amelia Island, where Katherine had just purchased a beach cottage. It would be the perfect place for our summer weekend getaway and a calm retreat for Sue. But, of course, our trips never went as smoothly as we had hoped. Matt and I were at our condo in St. Simon's the week before the planned trip. There, I could rent a van and drive to Amelia Island, only a few hours away, while the others would fly. So it made sense for me to drive. Until I went to rent the van. My driver's license had expired.

I rushed to the Department of Motor Vehicles, only to learn I had an even worse issue. They 'assured' me I could not get a new license in time to leave for Amelia Island by lunch. Finally, after begging and pleading, and even committing what one might call bribery, I walked out at half past eleven with a temporary license. It's amazing what a pair of gold earrings can do when you're desperate.

After a speedy trip, I was sitting in the Amelia airport parking lot when the ladies landed. As they exited, I blew the horn, pulled to the curb, and helped them load their luggage in the back. Following a stop for a fast-food lunch, we drove to Katherine's cute cottage, which was decorated in pastels with whitewashed furniture. The bedrooms were adorable and inviting as we each claimed a bed. We changed into shorts or swimsuits and walked along the beach while the four told me of their harrowing flight.

Apparently, they hit an air pocket as turbulence engulfed the plane, causing it to drop quickly as if it were literally falling from the sky. Once the pilot corrected the movement, they sat in quiet anticipation of another drop. Thankfully, none came, but Sue had already wet her pants when an overhead bin opened, and a briefcase fell out, hitting her head. The remainder of the flight was most uncomfortable, especially for her. But Sue was quite the trooper.

We decided to go antiquing the following morning. All of the chaos started when Katherine wanted to buy silver candelabras for her new antique sideboard back in Atlanta. Thus began the shopping spree that started a new trend. We began looking for specific items we all had a particular interest in and would choose one category for each trip. So, this trip was now based around silver. That morning we found silver prices extremely reasonable. Therefore, we all began thinking of places in our own homes that needed just the right sparkle of a silver piece or two. As we shopped, I found a silver coffee urn that would be such a stylish way to serve clients coffee at the office. Large silver trays were plentiful, so each of us purchased several. Katherine found her old English sterling candelabras. We found pitchers, beautiful bowls, salt and pepper shakers, a lovely mirror that was wonderfully French, and several unique items that we felt were important to our new collection. But, there was one issue. It was all tarnished.

Later that day, we returned to the cottage, stopping first to buy silver polish. That night we ordered pizza and started rubbing and buffing. "I know why this stuff was so cheap! It has to be polished!" Liz declared. That night was the only night of my life that I could ever say it was fun to polish silver. As midnight approached, we were getting giddy. I commented that we should probably leave by late morning so that I would have time to return the van and still join them on the flight. The polishing came to an abrupt halt. We all looked at one another.

Dorothy voiced what we were all thinking. "We're flying back. How on earth will we get all this silver through security?"

Breaking from her typical no-problem attitude, Liz looked like a deer in headlights. She shook her head and said, "Good, Lord! How in the hell did none of us think about that?" Then she began to laugh. Of course, not one of us had any idea how we would get our treasures home. But where there's a will, there's a way. We agreed and kept polishing.

The serious looks on the faces of the TSA Agents telling us to unpack every one of our bags for inspection nearly put us under. One even asked, "Where was the heist?" The travelers in line behind failed to appreciate the humor. It took forever for us to unpack each piece and repack it carefully once approved. But we wanted to ensure the new silver could make the trip home with as few dents as possible. What a mess. But we fell into hysterics when we were seated on the plane. All of a sudden, the silver catastrophe was actually funny.

Grab the Lace and Call Security!

Weeks rolled into months, and soon, we all needed another trip. Matt and I decided to buy a larger condo at St. Simon's. Alice now had a little boy, and Greg loved to bring friends. So we purchased a three-bedroom and said goodbye to the smaller two-bedroom unit. Following a little remodeling and sprucing up, the condo was ready for the ladies. Late spring at St. Simon's was full of several bazaars, antique fairs, and unusual shopping, so we planned our upcoming weekend around the island's calendar of events. Deciding to drive together, we enlisted Katherine's minivan, and on the trip down, we stopped for lunch. As we left the restaurant to return to highway 75, I spotted a warehouse with a huge sign that read, "Imports." I casually mentioned, "Doesn't that look like an interesting place to shop?"

Katherine hit the gas, crossed four lanes of traffic,

and screeched into the import's parking lot. Once we caught our breath, Liz laughed and said, "I understand why women become lesbians. My husband would have never done this for me."

I laughed, thinking of all the times I had seen interesting establishments along the roadside on various trips. It didn't matter how much I begged or pleaded. Matt kept on driving and would ask, "Did you say something?" as we zoomed on by. She was right. I didn't know a single man who would stop and cross all of those lines of traffic to shop. Matt's goal was more a Neanderthal idea of shopping—shoot it, bag it, and take it home. Whereas most women's ideas usually involved a bit more investigation.

With a few new treasures, we resumed our trip. After a leisurely Friday evening, we woke up early Saturday morning, ready to go. There was a bazaar in the park down near the village that opened at nine o'clock. As we walked around and looked at all of the antiques, gorgeous quilts, and unique handmade items, we spotted a tent full of exquisite laces of all kinds.

Now, I probably need to preface a little more about our shopping trips. Being a designer, whether my expertise was merited or not, before any of the ladies purchased anything, there was a familiar call when they held up their intended purchase. "Jan, do we love this?" would echo through the air. If I said yes, it was a go. If I hesitated in the least, they would put the item back down and walk away.

That morning, the tent with the laces had really caught my attention. I loved fancy hand towels hanging in my powder room and beautiful pillowcases on my guestroom bed. The more I thought, the more uses I imagined for that lace. As I picked up piece after piece, the group started to pay attention.

Liz was the first to voice her questions. "What in the hell are you going to do with all that?"

I began to paint a picture for her. "Can't you just see this hanging from the bottom of a monogrammed hand towel in my powder room?" I held up one of the lace pieces that almost looked crocheted. Then, picking up another delicate piece, I sighed and smiled as I expressed my visualization of it on the hem of sateen pillowcases.

Soon they had gotten the picture and were scooping up pieces of lace, calling, "Jan, do we love this one?"

By the time we left the bazaar, we each carried a shopping bag full of lace. After lunch in the village at St. Simon's, we were tired and returned to the condo. I suggested that everyone bring their lace from the car, and we could trim it for different uses.

That afternoon I fixed each of us a Fuzzy Navel and helped to cut the lace into useful pieces. As we worked, Liz brought out the iron and ironing board to press as we cut. Leaning over to gather more lace, she accidentally knocked over Sue and Katherine's glasses filled with the drinks made from our only supply of peach schnapps. Everybody grabbed the lace and started shaking the liquid off. We laughed at the expression on Liz's face as she cried, "Call security! I'll go quietly."

We all crashed in the living room that night after dinner, and no one wanted to see another piece of lace. But after a good night's sleep and talking on the way home the following day, we discovered the list of possibilities for our fine-looking laces was truly endless. Our lace trip had been a success.

On a busy Wednesday morning two weeks later, I got a call from Liz asking if I could meet her for lunch. Her voice sounded strange, not jovial like normal, and she indicated the meeting was important. Of course, my first thought was that the doctors decided they didn't like the color raspberry.

When I pulled up beside her car at Brio's, I saw Liz still waiting in the driver's seat. Before I could open my car door, she came around to the passenger side and slowly slid into the seat beside me. "Jan, I've got something to tell you. But I prefer it be just between us . . . for now. Bill and I have separated. He has his own apartment . . . with his new love. We've had issues for years, and now, they've become real problems. I haven't told a soul, but I can no longer deal with it by myself. The twins suspect something, although we tried to act normal when they come home." She began to cry.

From our conversation, it seemed that nothing in her life was smooth at this point. She was even considering a job change. I just listened but knew we needed to let the others know. Somehow, there was a better understanding of everything when we were all five involved; there was clarity when we discussed any issues together. Plus, I needed help guiding Liz's impulsive personality. I wanted help to convince her to take a long and careful look at her options. But, she disagreed with my group plan. I could tell she was hurting, which broke my heart.

"Liz, every marriage has its ups and downs," I began. "Maybe time will heal these wounds, and you certainly don't need to go through this and a job change simultaneously. You need more advice than just mine."

She finally agreed as we continued to try and bring some sanity to the multitude of issues she was facing. Her marriage, finances, the children, and her job — I could tell she was overwhelmed. Matt was out of town, and Greg was attending summer school for SAT prep, so I invited all the ladies to dinner that Thursday evening. At first, Dorothy wasn't sure if she could make it, but I explained it was mandatory and missing was not an option. Understanding, she assured me that she would be there.

· · ·

After dinner, Liz explained her circumstance. By the end of our time together that evening, the only clear message to Liz was that we loved her and were there to support her, but she was not to make any big decisions for at least three months. What we didn't know was that there was a situation waiting around that corner that none of us could help.

Our Original Has a Twin

Several weeks later, Matt had a meeting at Pebble Beach and asked if I wanted to join him. I was certainly not into golf, but I loved the little town of Carmel. Our group had been discussing the possibility of doing a little investing together. Katherine had suggested stocks and bonds; Sue had said buying gold was smart; Dorothy offered different charities and loved the idea of investing in humanity; Liz didn't care as long as we didn't buy any more silver or lace. And I suggested art because I had done rather well on several pieces I had purchased through a gallery in Georgetown. We were all instructed to pray about it, and so far, we hadn't spent a penny.

That week with Matt, I spent several days shopping in galleries in Monterey and Carmel. One afternoon on a stroll through Carmel, I saw a small sign with an arrow pointing down a cobblestone alley. Loving to explore, I followed the path. Not seeing anything in particular, I was ready to turn around when I heard voices behind a fence on the right. Curiosity got the best of me, and I decided to investigate.

Walking toward the sound of the laughter, I noticed a small iron gate. Peering through the wrought-iron design, I saw a simple little cottage. It was an art gallery that wasn't listed in any of the brochures I had collected. I opened the gate and followed the narrow brick walkway to a small porch with white benches on either side.

When I entered the gallery, I realized that all the artwork was done by a single artist, Thomas Kinkade. I had never heard of him before, but I could see that his work was exquisite. Every painting seemed full of a supernatural light. It was astounding to imagine how his brushes could create such impeccable brilliance. Through one of the sales assistants, I learned he was known as 'the painter of light.' It certainly made sense.

As I strolled around, taking in all of his different landscapes and scenes, my attention was drawn to one of his smaller works. I asked the young woman to tell me about the piece.

Smiling, she said, "You have good taste. That's an original. Mr. Kinkade painted it for a friend. Look, I can show you his inscription on the back." She gently removed the small painting and turned it over to show me a lantern drawn that read, "To the Christiansons, May your little light shine." As she rehung what she called a plein-air, she straightened the corners, and I noticed a plaque that read its title as *Mount Rundel.* It was a beautiful landscape of a majestic mountain. I asked the price and learned it was in the $12,000 range, which she said was a steal for one of his originals. A family had it in the gallery on consignment.

I could not get the plein-air off my mind for the next two days. Finally, I sent a text to the group with the price divided by five and a photo, asking if we would like this to be our first investment. Four texts came back within thirty minutes, each telling me to buy the painting. By the next afternoon, an investment club had begun.

When I returned to Atlanta, the group decided that Katherine would keep the painting because she had recently moved to a new house and needed art. We had no idea what to do with the new piece, but we were all excited as we had dinner at Katherine's and oohed and aahed over our purchase.

A month or so later, I was picking up linens at Phipps Plaza and saw there was a grand opening coming to the shop next to Saks. It was a Thomas Kinkade gallery. The door was open, and several people were beginning to hang art in what was to be the new gallery. I walked in and proudly announced, "Some friends and I own one of his originals."

The woman's face lit up as she asked, "May we borrow it for our grand opening?"

Thinking I should ask the others before I answered, I laughed. But then, I had a better idea. I assured the woman that we would be delighted for her to use the painting. I could feel the wheels turning as my mind formulated a plan while she explained how she would make a card stating that the painting was on loan. She insisted on listing the patrons' names, but I was just as insistent that the disclosure was totally unnecessary. I asked her to simply say it was on loan from an Atlanta investment club.

I knew Katherine never locked her house, and the only possible people there would be her two children and their nanny. I looked at my watch. They were probably still involved in their morning activities, and if I hurried, I could sneak the painting out of the house before they returned.

Pulling into Katherine's driveway, there was not a car in sight. As expected, I walked to the back door, which was unlocked. Tiptoeing in, I grabbed the painting from a bookcase in her living room and rushed back out. As I drove out of the neighborhood, I waved to her nanny and the children who were just passing through the gate. *That was close!*

· · ·

The open house was to take place in two weeks, so I called to arrange dinner for five at the Tavern at Phipps for the same night. As we ate, I casually mentioned that there was a rumor of a Thomas Kinkade gallery opening at Phipps. No one seemed too excited; they had already forgotten the artist who had painted our plein-air. So, to refresh their memory, I said, "You know, the artist that painted the piece we just bought."

Now they were excited. We decided to stop by the gallery after dinner. The gallery was crowded, and the staff served champagne as guests milled around, taking in the splendor of the master's work. I watched as Liz, not a big art fan, quickly made the rounds. On the other hand, Dorothy took her time and critiqued each piece. Katherine and Sue just meandered.

I quietly followed when Dorothy was near the area where our painting was on display. She suddenly stopped and called to Katherine, "Come, look at this. Does this look familiar to you?"

Katherine moved closer to the painting and said, "The plaque reads *Mount Rundel*." She called for Sue to join them.

Now the three of them were in full discussion as Katherine assured them our painting was in her book-case. Watching their eyes grow bigger, I had never been so tickled. They softly called for Liz, and I could tell they were looking for me.

Liz walked up and said, "Thank the Lord. Are we

ready to go?" She had had enough art for one night. They showed her their find, and she stopped abruptly and started looking around. "Where is Jan? That's not ours. Ours is an original, and that means one." She looked again. "We've been had! Our original has a twin."

"Look! It says it's on loan by another group in Atlanta," Sue fussed.

I walked up, trying hard not to laugh. "What's going on?" I managed to ask, seemingly oblivious to the piece.

"What's the name of our original?" Katherine asked.

"*Mount Rundel*," I answered.

"Oh my goodness, we've been taken. If there are two in Atlanta, how many are there across the country?" Dorothy asked.

In an adamant tone, Liz declared, "We're suing that gallery!"

By then, I was about to wet my pants. All four were talking at once about the action we needed to take to restore our honor.

A voice chimed in, "This must be the group that you were telling me about, Jan! We want to thank you all so much for loaning us your exceptional piece."

I burst out laughing as I watched their faces go from devastation to exhilaration. The young sales assistant asked for everyone's attention in the gallery and then introduced us as the owners of this fine original. As the group beamed and each was handed another glass of champagne, I didn't fail to notice the occasional glares through the laughter. None of us knew how vital the laughter from our shenanigans would be in the year to follow.

An Unexpected Decision

Now, remember how I mentioned that Liz had already made a decision, a rather big one? It was almost Christmas again, and I was just finding out the extent of her thought process. Her divorce was now final, and she was in love.

Tom was tall, dark, and handsome in a rugged sort of way. He was an engineer that she met during the construction work on the PICU. When they first met, it was on the occasion of Liz chewing him out over a pretty big mistake with the electrical and oxygen outlets. Two days later, he had marched into her office, showing that his drawings had not been correctly transferred to the architectural drawings. He indicated she should call her architect if she wanted to raise hell with anyone.

After checking with the architect, Liz realized she owed Tom an apology. Doing so, she suggested that she owed him dinner as well. He had smiled and offered that very evening. At dinner, Liz learned that Tom had lost his first wife in a skiing accident several years before. The two had never had children, and he had no interest in remarriage, but a courtship began that evening. It had not been easy, simply because Liz and Bill still had two things needing resolution— the sadness of their girls and what they wanted to do about their house.

Therefore, she and Tom were taking things slowly, and she had yet to introduce him to her girls. With the upheaval of the divorce, Liz decided they needed more time before meeting a new man in her life. I had met Tom once when Liz and I were doing a walk-through of the new PICU, although he didn't realize I knew what was happening between them.

As I walked over to discuss an out-of-place petition wall with the architect, Tom and Liz disappeared. Finally locating the pair in what was to be the nurse's lounge, I laughed as Tom appeared to be wearing lipstick. I pulled a tissue from my purse, handed it to Tom, and pointed to his lips.

He quickly wiped off the red, glanced at Liz, and laughed as he said, "My goodness! Where did that come from?"

We laughed together as I looked over at Liz. But just then, she suddenly grabbed her side and said, "That was a sharp pain! I need some lunch."

Tom took her hand and asked, "You okay?"

She took a deep breath and said, "I should be after I eat. I'm starved."

It was weeks later that I saw Liz again when the five of us went out for dinner. She didn't look good; she looked tired. But that couldn't explain the feeling I had. It was as if her personality had changed entirely, not in a bad way, but in a different way. I chalked it up to the divorce and other issues with her girls, plus her home was fairly large with a pool, and both required a lot of attention. Then there was the whole hospital being in flux with crews working everywhere. Liz's plate was more than full.

Sue asked, "Liz, are you okay? You sure are quiet tonight."

She shrugged and passed off the concern, saying, "I'm fine. Just tired."

But Dorothy added, "Liz, did you know Tom Wheeler goes to our church?"

Liz nodded. "I did know that."

"He's such a nice man," Dorothy continued. "I'm glad you two have become friends."

That comment opened up the floodgate to numerous questions. The sparkle returned to Liz's eyes. "He's a good man, y'all. You'll love him, and I would like for you to meet him soon. He has access to his company's house on a lake in Georgia and says we'll have to use it for one of our weekends. Unfortunately, there's no shopping in sight."

Sue asked, "How serious is this, Liz?"

"Well, I have no intention of jumping from the frying pan into the fire," Liz answered, "and I haven't mentioned anything to my girls. But it's nice. Being by yourself can be so lonely. Sue, I don't know how you've done it all these years."

Sue shrugged her shoulders. "There are times I think about dating, but I think back, and I just couldn't go through another season like the first."

Katherine jumped in and said, "Well, Liz, I'm glad you found somebody to hang out with. And Sue, one day, it's going to happen for you. Mark my words."

Dorothy chuckled. "And we can make honest women of you two in five minutes! Frank and I are always prepared for a quickie wedding."

We all laughed and decided to visit Frank and Dorothy's church on Sunday. They were thinking of redecorating their sanctuary and needed a few tips.

Liz smiled. "Decorating tips, my ass! Y'all just want to meet Tom!" She knew us too well.

You're Going to Put Your Eyes Out!

Everybody met in Conyers Sunday morning. Liz had gotten there early and was standing in the vestibule with Tom. As we were all introduced, he said, "I feel like I know each of you from Liz's non-stop talking about your unbelievable trips."

The music started. We entered and walked up to Tom's favorite pew. The sanctuary was actually very nice; the only things that looked worn were the cornices and drapery panels on either side of the six windows. When asked for my input on sprucing things up, I mentioned the panels, and I'm not sure whether Liz had a temporary brain kink or was trying to impress Tom, but she volunteered us to make the new panels. She was a decent seamstress, as was Dorothy, but the rest of us couldn't even sew on a button.

After having lunch at the lake house with Frank and Dorothy and our new friend, Tom, we planned a meeting for the following weekend to make draperies. We planned to meet at Liz's, and I was to order the fabric. Dorothy and Liz would each have their sewing machines ready, and Katherine was tasked with securing the lining. Sue was to bring straight pins and every pair of scissors she could find.

After sending photos of seven different fabrics, we agreed on a soft, olive-green patterned velvet. It seemed simple enough; we assumed the pattern would be easy to match. And with all six panels being the same size, we were confident the job would be a cinch. When the fabric arrived, I took a sample to buy thread and a special tape that was supposed to make it easier to pinch-pleat. I had a friend with a woodworking business who said he could make the six wooden cornices we needed since the old ones had fallen apart as they were removed.

I picked the cornices up Saturday morning, and we were ready to start our project. The only one who had ever upholstered anything was Dorothy. She enlisted my help, and the other three began the work on the panels. Now when you upholster cornices, you first cut a layer of padding. We decided to glue the padding to the wood, which worked remarkably well. It was the next step that caused the problem. You have to staple the fabric tightly over the padding. I had never used an electric stapler, and neither had Dorothy. That had always been Frank's job.

Plugging the stapler in, Dorothy said, "I'll do my

side first." Squeezing the handle of the stapler, we heard the shot. But when she removed the gun, there was no staple in the fabric. We tried it several more times. Still no staple anywhere.

Every time we'd shoot the gun, we heard a strange click. Finally, Dorothy yelled for Liz, "This staple gun is broken!"

"I just used it last week. It works fine," Liz defended.

"Well, it's not working now," I chimed in. Dorothy and I were both getting irritated at wasting time.

The sewing machine stopped, and Liz appeared in the garage where we were working. Dorothy said, "I'll show you!" She reshot the gun.

Liz screamed, "Stop! You have it upside down! You're going to put your eye out!" She told Dorothy to go sew on the sewing machine and that she and I would do the cornices. After another thirty minutes of total frustration with me, she fumed, "Leave the cornices. I'll do them myself later. Just come with me to help with the panels."

I followed her inside and tried to keep my opinions to myself.

"Do you know how to thread a needle?" Liz asked me.

I had taken a two-day sewing class in college. So, of course, I knew how to thread a needle. I cut about a six-inch piece of thread, threaded the needle, and said, "I'm ready."

Liz shook her head. "Good grief! You need a lot more thread than that to hem the entire side of a panel."

I turned and watched what Sue was doing and cut my thread accordingly. As Katherine had cut the lining pieces too big, each side of the panels had to be double-hemmed so as not to show the lining at the seams. As I began to seam the side of my panel, my stitches ranged from an eighth of an inch to two full inches, which caused serious gapping.

Liz walked over, took my needle, and cut the thread off with her scissors. She then removed my thread from the panel. Bringing over one of Sue's panels, she calmly suggested that I was to follow that example as best I could.

Looking around, I didn't see any more green thread, so I picked up a cream-colored spool instead, thinking that it wouldn't make any difference since it was on the back. Glancing up, I saw that Katherine and Sue looked as frustrated as I was. This day was a much bigger undertaking than we had anticipated. But I was used to big projects, so I knew we could work it out. I merely needed to concentrate and not talk anymore.

I was so proud when I finally finished hemming the side of the panel. The stitches looked even, but when I turned it over, the cream thread had penetrated the green velvet all the way down the fabric. I excused myself, supposedly, to go to the restroom and ran to my car. I kept an installation kit in my trunk, which contained everything Jordan Designs would ever need for mistakes that commonly occurred on design firm jobs. I found touchup paint in multiple colors, including olive green.

I got a small artist's brush and the little paint bottle and snuck back inside. I picked up my panel and went to the kitchen table, hopefully out of everyone's sight. Laying the panel out, I painted the cream-colored thread a close match to the green velvet. As I was finishing the paint on the last two stitches, Liz walked in.

"What are you doing?" she yelled.

"Fixing my panels. What do you think?"

"You're painting your panel?"

"No. Just little bits of thread."

By this time, everyone else had come running to see what was happening. Katherine cried, "We are not capable of this. I quit!"

I thankfully said, "Me too."

Sue sat down on the kitchen floor with her head in her hands. "It's six o'clock, and we've done half of two panels . . . that look like crap."

Liz walked over to the phone and called two sisters she knew who had made their life's work fabricating draperies. Then, after hanging up, she said, "They'll charge seventy-five a panel and fifty per cornice."

I had never been so relieved. I would have sold my car to have paid those two blessed ladies.

. . .

Two Sundays later, we stood in the church to be recognized for creating the beautiful new draperies on the windows. I felt like we were cheating in church, but I was more than thankful that the drapery fiasco was over. I never planned to thread another needle as long as I lived. That's the day I truly understood the meaning of a saying I had heard my whole life, "The road to hell is paved with good intentions."

Bagpipes, Are You Serious?

⟡

Matt and I left for the beach on Friday. He had a golfing meeting at Sea Island that Saturday, so we figured we could sneak in a weekend for the two of us, and I'd fly back on Monday, as he needed to stay for more meetings.

My phone rang at six-thirty on Sunday morning. It was lying on the bedside table closest to Matt. Picking it up, he rolled over, with his eyes still closed, and handed it to me. I cleared my throat and whispered, "Hello."

"Well, Lilly died last night," Liz began. "Sue has taken to her bed, and we're having a meeting to plan the funeral." She sounded disgusted. "You're not going to believe this funeral. Sue wants bagpipers to come out of the woods playing *Amazing Grace*. She's already decided who'll be pallbearers, and she wants a luncheon afterward!" She huffed, "Does she have any idea how much this is going to cost? And how much work it'll be for all of us? For a dog . . . a three-pound dog?"

"Liz, you know how Sue is," I tried to interject. "Lilly is all she had. That dog was her child."

Still annoyed, Liz fussed, "Well, I'm so glad you feel that way! Because we need you to fly in today and bring the box that you bought at the Paris flea market."

"What?" I sat up in the bed, no longer whispering but thankful that Matt was a heavy sleeper. "What do you need that box for?" I couldn't imagine what she was talking about.

"Sue said she knew you wouldn't mind because that box was the perfect size to bury Lilly in. But she wants it painted pink."

"Painted? Pink? You can't be serious! That box dates back to the eighteen hundreds, and I paid a fortune for it." Now, I was disgusted.

"Well," Liz's voice was now dripping with sarcasm. "Just remember, it's all Sue has. That dog is her child." Then she fumed, "Bring the damn box and get here as soon as you can. Oh yes, we're to walk behind the pallbearers, pushing a pink baby carriage with all of Lilly's toys. She wants those put in the grave with Lilly at the last minute. So . . . we need a pink pillowcase, if you happen to have one, to wrap the pillow in the box.

Sue is having a viewing tomorrow night. That is . . . if she can leave her bed."

"Good grief!" I mumbled.

"Dorothy is working on all of the music," Liz continued to explain. "And Katherine is getting wine and cheese for the viewing while that dog lies in state. In a pink tutu . . . with pink ribbons in her hair. Sue took the portrait of Lilly off her wall, and we're to put it on an easel beside the box."

"Oh, Liz. I hate this for Sue. But this is ridiculous! I've never been to a funeral for a person like the one you're describing."

She threw my words back at me again in a 'yeah-yeah' sort of way. "Oh, but just remember. Lilly was all she had! So we need to shut up and make this happen, or she'll have a conniption and be in her bed forever."

Shaking my head, I asked, "What do Dorothy and Katherine have to say about this funeral idea?"

"Dorothy has Frank officiating, and he said it'd be fine because he believes animals go to heaven. And you know Katherine . . . she's just hoping it won't get written up in the paper."

"I'll try to be there by this afternoon," I promised as I yawned. Of course, Matt was never going to believe all of this. He was snoring lightly beside me, and I knew he'd have a heart attack if he had any idea what I paid for that box. Three-thousand dollars and two-hundred years of history was to be buried.

My Beautiful Box

Telling Matt as little as possible, I made my reservation and was in the air four hours later. Upon landing, I rented a car and drove to the cemetery where we were supposed to meet. I must have been the first to arrive because I didn't see a soul. However, within minutes, I heard a horn blaring as a car drove up behind me. Looking in my rearview mirror, I recognized Katherine's car. Liz was riding shotgun. They pulled up alongside, and Liz lowered her window and asked, "Have you got the box?"

I nodded.

"We have a tarp and pink paint. The funeral director said we could paint it in the back parking lot. Follow us," she ordered. Katherine pulled off.

Taking one turn after another, it occurred to me that we were not in a pet cemetery. I noted the mausoleums and tombstones, and by then, I was getting a headache. I was hungry, tired, and now more than annoyed. I still couldn't believe we were doing all this for that dog.

Pulling into a parking space, I walked to the other side and grabbed the box. Katherine and Liz were already spreading out the tarp. I looked at my beautiful box, or should I say, coffin, and yelled to the other two, "This is crazy! Lilly would have fit in a shoe box. Or at least a boot box."

Katherine put her hand over her mouth in shock and mumbled, "Don't ever let Sue hear you say that."

"It's just a box, for God's sake!" Liz fussed. "Get over it! It's probably cursed, anyway. You know how they were in the eighteenth century."

After laying the box on the tarp, we gave each other hugs and began to laugh. Katherine took a spray paint can with a pink top out of a Home Depot bag and said, "I hope none of my clients see this on social media. They'll take their accounts away in a New York minute . . . thinking I've lost my mind. I considered wearing a ski mask."

Liz looked at Katherine. "Just take the top off and shake the can good." By now, Liz had had it with all of the crazy arrangements. She just wanted to get the whole ordeal over and be done.

Katherine began to spray soft pink onto my ancient mahogany box. When she finished spraying the first coat on the outside, she opened the lid. "No!" I yelled. "Why do we have to paint the inside? By the time we put the pink pillow in, you won't even see the inside."

Liz walked over and grabbed my shoulders. "Jan, it's going in the ground! What damn difference does it make?" She looked back over to Katherine and shouted, "Spray!"

Taking a second spray can from the bag, she shook it and began to cover the inside with that horrible shade of pink. She stopped and focused her eyes straight on mine. "Crap. It's not sticking."

We watched as two large areas of the box began to peel. Liz looked up and said, "I told you this damn thing was haunted. How could something this easy be this hard? We should have sanded it before we started."

I bowed up and threatened, "I'll put it back in my car before I let you use a piece of sandpaper on that box!"

Two hours later, with redo's, the paint adhered in all but two small spots. But they were right in front. I promised to get some pink contact paper and cut out pieces in the shapes of flowers to serve as patches.

After letting the box dry, we took it inside to the funeral director. He waved his hand over his nose, looking shocked. "Phew! It smells like paint!"

With no desire to discuss the ruined box any further, Liz shook her head and said, "Duh! It's just been painted. And don't worry about the spots. We have it under control." She looked at me and added, "Don't we, Jan?"

"Do you realize what a problem you are causing for me?" he asked, still waving his hands in front of his nose. "This is the first time we've ever permitted a pet to be buried on a family plot." He sighed and added, "But I was concerned Miss Sue would join Lilly if we said no. She assured me it would just be a few close friends and a quiet service."

Liz looked at me and mouthed, "Oh, hell," and then the word, "bagpipes."

All This and Amazing Grace

After stopping by to console Sue and being told by Dorothy that she was still too distraught to take visitors, Katherine, Liz, and I went out to dinner and to shop for a pink pillowcase and contact paper. Then, driving home, we stopped for the wine, cheese, and nuts for a viewing that would take place the following evening.

While looking for the supplies, a case of giggles came upon us as we relived the day. Liz hadn't seen the humor in any of it and had gone home to work on her medical reports due in the morning. The hospital had bought two new buildings, and she was on overload. Sue had been bedridden since Lilly took her last breath. And Dorothy and her sweet husband, Frank, were trying to plan a eulogy for an unsaved, spoiled rotten, three-pound dog.

Once back at her house, Katherine and I began

cutting the flower shapes from the contact paper and polished the silver trays and bowls for the snacks. Just then, Dorothy called with another assignment. "We're going to need twelve pink boutonnieres."

"Boutonnieres?" Katherine asked. "What on earth for?"

Sue explained, "Two for the bagpipers, one for Frank, and nine men in her family are pallbearers."

"What are they going to 'bear'? The box? And that takes nine men?" I asked.

"Just do it," Dorothy cried. By now, she'd hit her limit as well.

I shook my head. *Just stay cool. This too shall pass*, I thought to myself.

All was ready for the viewing by three o'clock the following afternoon. Well, almost. The cut-out contact flowers were lovely, but they didn't stick. So Katherine ran out to buy super-glue, which did the trick. And the only pillowcase we were able to locate had little ballerinas on it, but we felt it worked since they were dressed in tutus like Lilly.

The funeral director, who we now knew as Charlie, suggested we wait in the vestibule as they took Lilly inside first. I certainly don't mean to sound callous, but Lilly didn't even look dead when we looked in the box. Her eyes were closed, and she looked like herself since she had spent her typical days sleeping.

My designer eyes thought the bows in her hair seemed too big for the pink tutu, and I figured that would bother Sue. After a brief argument, we decided to cut them down to mimic her typical bows. Neither Katherine nor I wanted to touch Lilly, so Liz worked on the ribbons and whispered, "Good grief! Go sit down."

When Liz had finished the task, she started to walk over to join us but forgot about the step down from the platform where Lilly rested. Her foot stepped into thin air, and Liz invented a new dance move while trying to keep her balance. She hit the pew full force where we were sitting as she turned in mid-air and plopped down.

Seeing that Liz wasn't hurt, Katherine and I went into hysterics. Liz stared at us, laughing and crying all at once, gradually giving way to her own laughter. All of this over a little dog. We tried but couldn't regain our composure when Charlie walked in. He shot us a look signaling reprimand and turned to walk back out. We just kept laughing. We knew he was thinking, *how could they be so insensitive?*

The next couple of hours were spent preparing the food and drinks for the viewing. As we worked, we'd start laughing all over again whenever our eyes met. Not small giggles, but belly laughs. I must have made a dozen trips to the ladies' room, and the more we laughed, the funnier it got.

Thankfully, we got the silliness out of our system

before Sue walked in and screamed, "Where's the portrait?"

Dorothy and Frank had the big pink easel and Lilly's likeness in their car. He ran out, brought it in, and we set it at the foot of the box. When Sue walked over to the box and looked inside, her knees buckled, but we caught her just in time. Liz shouted, "We need smelling salts!"

I had an old sample of perfume in my purse, grabbed it, and put it under Sue's nose. It had been in my purse for probably five years and could have brought the dead back to life. Finally, Sue regained her composure and sat down in the front row with the four of us.

We had set up a guestbook in the vestibule along with two bouquets of pink roses. Two more arrangements were in the viewing room, at the head and the foot of the box. In a small room off to the side, on a beautifully draped table showcasing a pink satin tablecloth, sat silver trays, and bowls for the small reception. Rosé wine sat in a silver champagne bucket with crystal wine glasses and pink napkins engraved with the name Lilly sat close by. All was ready.

Sue sat quietly, dabbing her eyes with a lace handkerchief. Liz nudged me and asked, "What will we do if no one shows, and does the lace on that handkerchief look familiar?"

"How many people were called?" I asked, and then nodded yes to her lace question.

"Dorothy handled that. I don't know," Liz replied.

We noticed Dorothy fidgeting and looking around. It was nearly time; the viewing was from six to eight, and only the five of us were there. About a quarter after, people began to meander into the room; no one we knew, but they all knew Sue and must have understood how special Lilly was to that woman. We were delighted that nearly fifty tender hearts came to say goodbye to Lilly over the evening.

As the three of us packed up the remaining refreshments, we heard Sue and Dorothy talking. It was a sweet time for the two of them, and Sue hugged Dorothy as she whispered, "Look how many people loved Lilly."

The funeral was at eleven the following day. It had rained overnight, but the daylight had brought puffy, white clouds and plenty of sunshine. Nine pallbearers walked reverently to the open grave and put Lilly's box on a draped serving cart. Several friends had sent flowers, and Sue had a spray of pink roses ordered to lie on the top of the box. To be honest, the gravesite really looked beautiful.

We had walked behind the pallbearers, pushing Lilly's baby carriage as instructed. But with the earlier rain, that carriage bogged down further and further with every push. Liz finally walked to the front of the carriage and picked it up to carry it the rest of the way. We placed it beside the gravesite when the bagpipers commenced their march from the nearby woods playing *Amazing Grace*. The pastor had the shortest eulogy in the history of a funeral. It went a bit like this: Father, thank you for the comfort Lilly has given Sue all these years. We thank you that the Bible speaks of white horses in heaven, which gives us great hope of Lilly's arrival there and the confidence that she and Sue will be united one day for eternity. Amen.

I looked around and counted about thirty people sitting under the tent; we had ordered lunch for eighty. But we figured it would be okay. Sue was oblivious as we quickly hid forty plates of food.

That night we all sacrificed our normal chat time together as we allowed Sue to bask in the events of the last two days. Then, just before retiring for bed, Sue asked if we thought she should get another dog. Liz laughed, took Sue's hand, and then as sweetly as possible for her, said, "I think that answer is going to take some thought."

The next day, I flew back to St. Simon's in mourning - over my now pink Parisian box.

Dixie Cups

After the 'funeral,' I was slammed at work. But, wouldn't you know, Liz called in a panic. "Can you go shopping with me one day this week? I'll explain later."

"Sure. I can go Wednesday or Thursday late. Where are we going?" I asked.

"I'll explain later!" Liz said as she chuckled. "I'll pick you up at your office around five on Wednesday if that works. We'll grab some dinner and then shop a little."

When I got to the office on Monday morning, I had a message from Valerie. She was not feeling well and wouldn't be in this week. Calling in sick was not like her, and I began to worry. Then I got a call from her mother. Valerie's husband had committed suicide. I remembered that Valerie had been mentioning that he was suffering from one migraine after another. Her mother explained that he had been diagnosed with an inoperable brain tumor on Friday and had hung himself Saturday morning. They found a note that indicated he didn't want to put his wife through everything the doctor had warned him would happen as the tumor grew. Valerie was devastated, and as most wives would have done, she blamed herself.

I left the office immediately and drove over to her apartment. I'll always remember that afternoon as one of the hardest of my life. But Valerie's faith made it bearable. Her pastor had assured her that depression and hopelessness were as much a sickness as his tumor. Therefore, she could rest assured that her husband was with Jesus.

After making certain Valerie was as okay as possible, I went home. But that night, I snuggled up to Matt a little closer, grateful for our lives and our children. I realized how fast things could change, and I promised myself to slow down a little and pay more attention to the most important parts of my life. It saddened me to think how often I had neglected to follow that resolution. I then remembered my busy week at the office and how I had considered earlier that the shopping trip with Liz might have to wait. Yes, I definitely needed to make some changes. I'd rearrange some appointments to spend time with

Valerie and still go shopping with Liz. I kissed Matt on his cheek and closed my eyes.

The funeral was scheduled for Wednesday at three. I checked with Liz, and we moved our shopping date to Thursday. I was so proud of our office because every staff member was at the church to support their co-worker. All had signed up to prepare meals that would last for several weeks. I told Valerie to take the time she needed as we could cover her projects; we'd see her when she was ready. The look on her face broke my heart, and I cried for her pain as I walked to my car.

Our office was back in rhythm by Thursday morning, though the atmosphere still held an element of sadness. I was thankful that I could look forward to shopping with Liz later that day. It was difficult to be sad with her; no one could lift my spirits like that woman. I was waiting outside when Liz pulled up at four. I knew to be right ready because Liz was never even one second late. As we drove to Phipps Plaza, I told her all about Valerie. Listening compassionately, she assured me that her hospital would send flowers the following day.

Then she explained the shopping expedition. "Jan,

Tom has asked me to go away with him for the weekend. He wants to go to Cashiers to a cabin his firm owns." She laughed and added, "He could tell I was a little nervous about a weekend trip and assured me I had nothing to worry about. It would just be a nice time for us to get to know each other better. So I'm going. And here's my dilemma . . . I need some fancy underwear and night-gowns." She grinned. "I'd like to get to know him better too, so I think I need to be prepared . . . just in case."

"Why Liz Moore! What have you got on your mind?" I teased.

She merely shrugged and said, "I'm not quite sure."

After grabbing a hamburger at the Grille, we ended up in the lingerie section at Saks. Searching rack after rack, we found lovely nightgowns, cozy robes, and gorgeous bras and panties. Then I sat in the dressing area, waiting for Liz to come out. I waited and waited and waited. Finally, I knocked on the door, "Do you need some help?"

The door opened slowly. "Look at this!" Liz muttered. She was standing in a red nightgown, and you need to remember that both of us were already in our fifties. Body parts had made drastic changes in location, and Liz had big boobs. They were now closer to her waist than the center of her chest, nowhere near where the gown had been designed to hold them. She shook her head. "I look like an old cow! And look at my nipples. They're the size of the bottom of a Dixie cup!" She attempted to push them higher. "What am I going to do? This is awful."

I tried not to laugh, but she did look funny. And not the least bit sexy. "You stay right here, and I'll be back in a jiffy."

"See if you can find the moo-moo section!" she yelled as I left the dressing room.

I was shopping for an entirely different style when I reached the rack. And then I saw it. There was a gown that looked like a shirt with buttons up the front. It was sheer and a beautiful shade of green, perfect for Liz's new shade of auburn hair. Then I found a lace bra and panties in the exact same shade of green. Knowing how upset she was when I left her in that dressing room, I hurried back.

I rushed in and handed her the bra and panties first. "Put these on."

She huffed. "I need a nightgown!"

"Put those on!" I ordered. "I'll be right outside."

In just a few minutes, she opened the door. "These are nice," she admitted.

Then I handed her the long-sleeved sheer flowing gown. I started with the buttons at the bottom, and she started at the top. When I stepped back, Liz looked in the mirror.

"Jan, this is just right!" She looked sexy and much more comfortable with her reflection. "Go get some more," she bossed. By closing time, Liz was ready for her weekend.

On the way back to the office to get my car, she said, "You know, I may not need any of this stuff."

"That might be true," I agreed. "But, it's better to have it and not need it than to need it and not have it."

I saw Liz again the following week, and I'm sure she could read the questions in my eyes. She just tossed her head and said, "That man loves green!"

We're in Serious Trouble

◌◌

Tom and Liz spent the next year getting to know each other quite well. They had even taken a European cruise. On that vacation, they returned by way of Istanbul, where they had bought several oriental rugs for Liz's new lake house, plus a box of Cuban cigars. As they were leaving the ship, Tom casually mentioned that bringing the cigars into the United States might be illegal. "No problem," Liz said. "I can put them out of sight. I'll just stick them in my bra." Taking them out of the box, she placed them around the large cups of her bra. But as the two walked toward customs, they saw police officers with dogs. With utmost sincerity, Liz turned to Tom and said, "This is the only time in my life I've hoped the odor of my crotch will attract more attention than the smell of Cuban cigars."

• • •

As Liz related this story to the four of us, we couldn't imagine what Tom must have been thinking. But, we realized by now that he was just as much in love and seemed to anticipate what would come out of Liz's mouth in time to prepare.

Sharing more about their trip, Liz explained that she had several instances of a sharp pain that coursed through her side. Apparently, it was so severe that it nearly took her to her knees. So she had made a doctor's appointment to get it checked.

Of course, my first question was, "When is your appointment?"

It was the following week at ten o'clock on Thursday. Katherine, Dorothy, Sue, and I met Liz that morning for breakfast and escorted her to the doctor's office afterward. It seemed like we waited for hours, assuring ourselves that everything was fine. She had probably just eaten something strange on that ship that didn't agree with her.

But then her doctor, Dr. Matthews, who happened to be a client of Jordan Designs, came to the door and shook his head. The look on his face spoke volumes. We knew we were in trouble. Liz followed him out and tried to be cheerful as she explained, "I need a lot more tests." Then tears rolled down her cheeks. "They're pretty sure it's ovarian cancer."

I remember Katherine saying, "Doctors don't know everything."

It was as if her words gave the rest of us a lifeline to hold onto, and we each quickly agreed. We were not going to believe any of this; Liz just needed more tests. She was going to be fine. Doctors make mistakes all the time. But I knew this gynecologist; he was not an alarmist and was very conservative in all of his diagnoses.

I spent that night with Liz. As we talked and wondered and hoped, we thought back over funny times and occasionally laughed, but inside, there was a fear we both tried so hard to ignore.

Tests after tests came back, affirming Dr. Matthew's suspicion. By then, I had researched ovarian cancer from stem to stern, and most of what I had read brought no comfort. But every now and then, there were stories about women beating this disease. If anyone was strong enough to beat this, it was Liz. I'd always heard the phrase, "There comes a time in everyone's life when they face the dark night of the soul." The five of us faced that night together. And the closeness we had felt before paled in comparison to the bond we had now formed.

· · ·

The first thing we did was create a shared calendar to make sure that one of us was with Liz for every single test, appointment, or consultation. Next, we started shopping for wigs, cute hats, and anything else we could think of that would help ease Liz's concern about losing her hair. We tried to turn every negative into a positive as the news grew progressively worse.

Finally, they scheduled surgery to de-bulk her tumors. The four of us sat with Tom that day. We wanted to talk. We needed to talk. But we sat in silence. The hours ticked by as we waited for any news. *Were they able to get it all? Would she actually need the chemo they already had planned? Would there be the miracle so many were praying for?*

Her surgeon finally came to the waiting room, showing evidence of the long surgery in each of his slow steps. He had personally known Liz for years. His face was void of expression, and we knew it was not a good sign. With a trembling voice, he said, "Cancer cells fell like snowflakes. I did the best I could. We'll start chemo as soon as she's able."

I walked up and took his hands as my tears flowed. "Thank you." I turned to the rest of our group. No one knew what to say; we were all in disbelief.

Katherine pulled out the calendar. "I'll take the first chemo treatment. Who'll take the second?" And that's how the rest of our months played out.

· · ·

When Liz's chemotherapy treatments began, we sat with her, held her head, cried, and laughed. There's no way to explain the myriad of emotions we shared over those months of chemo. But finally, the first round was over.

By then, Liz had at least ten new wigs and felt slightly better. She had decided to temporarily move to her lake house where she felt the calmness of nature. She loved the water and could be with her girls when they were home. The problem with this plan was that the lake house was not in Atlanta. It was fairly far from her doctors and us, but we were determined to make it work.

Matt and I had sold our house to downsize and bought an apartment in a high-rise in Atlanta, which just happened to be close to the hospital. Matt was still traveling a lot, leaving plenty of opportunities for me to care for Liz. She could be at her lake house in north Georgia but stay with me at our apartment for any doctor's appointments or necessary tests. We figured that was the better of two worlds.

The four of us and our calendars had everything covered, or so we thought. In the middle of this, in a typical Liz way, she had decided to redecorate her lake house. She wanted to throw out all the old furniture and move everything from her home in Atlanta out to the lake. I freaked. She had no clue of what she was attempting to undertake. In her weakened state from the chemo, there was no way she could handle such an endeavor. But, as we all researched the calendar, the four of us got it scheduled. The key was to do it all without Liz.

After talking with Liz's children and some other scheming, we scheduled the move for the following weekend. I'd go up to the lake early with one of Liz's charities, pull out everything we didn't need in the new plan, and get it donated and loaded in their truck. I scheduled from eleven to one that day for the loading. The other trucks were to arrive with the unloading from one to three. They were to get beds set up, furniture and rugs in place, and stack what looked to be close to eighty boxes back in the kitchen. The group would arrive at three, and we had until four o'clock on Sunday to finish the job. Tom and Liz's twins were bringing her out at that time.

I'll never forget the look on everyone's faces when they saw the multitude of boxes. We decided we needed an assembly line. Katherine and Sue were to unpack the boxes. Dorothy was to put things going into cabinets into their proper places. I was to accessorize. The lake house was a two-story, and I was sure I had not worn enough deodorant as we climbed the stairs and carried so many boxes to the various cabinets and drawers throughout. I don't believe any of us had ever worked that hard to meet a rather insane deadline.

Early Saturday, I grabbed Sue to take over Dorothy's job, leaving poor Katherine by herself with forty more boxes. Dorothy could sew, and we needed a shower curtain. So I handed her two drapery panels and said, "We need you to make a shower curtain right now."

Dorothy tilted her head and frowned. "I don't have a sewing machine."

"Improvise," I said as I turned and walked out.

By nightfall, Dorothy had pinch-pleated panels turned into gathered panels on a shower rod, but I didn't think they looked quite right. So I brought another of the same drapery panels and asked her to make a top treatment for a second rod. If looks could have killed, I would not be writing this today. But she did it, and how, I will never know. It even had a ruffle along the bottom.

By four in the morning, we had all the boxes unloaded, most everything had a new home, and Katherine was in Liz's closet, fussing that there was no room for all her shoes. I gave her a look and repeated my instructions, "Improvise."

We slept in one-hour shifts that night, except for poor Dorothy. I don't believe she ever got her turn. But by noon on Sunday, and after fifteen cups of coffee, flower arrangements were placed, a throw was casually draped on her sofa, lamps were glowing, and every room whispered, "Welcome." We were thrilled that Liz's Atlanta furniture worked so nicely at the lake. Katherine had even put cinnamon sticks and cloves in a pot on the stove to add a pleasant fragrance to our design and, I feared, to cover body odor. In my career, I have completed a lot of projects. But none has ever, or will ever be, as important as this one. It was for Liz, and it had to be flawless.

I'm sure Liz believed she was walking into a huge mess Sunday afternoon when she saw our cars. But she really had no idea what a beautiful home she was entering. Truly, Liz came home to the perfect placement of everything special in her life, including us.

What Have Y'all Done? A 38 What?

When Liz walked into the lake house, we were all sitting, reading different forms of literature with one hand and sipping wine with the other. Katherine spoke first. "So glad you could join us! It's so relaxing here."

Liz looked around and burst into tears. "What have y'all done?" she asked.

"We've come to welcome you home," Dorothy answered.

Sue walked over and took Liz's hand. "Would you like a tour?"

We all followed as Sue led Liz through every room. We watched her expressions as she saw that all the beds were made up beautifully, draperies were hung down to the new ruffled shower curtain, her closets were organized, and everything was in place.

As I stood back, I could see that the weight of the world had been lifted from Liz's shoulders. What she had dreaded was already completed. We had moved her in, lock, stock, and barrel. She was home.

Speaking of barrels, that night in the quiet of the evening, we realized just how out of the way her lake house sat. We couldn't even see the light from another cottage. "Do you have a gun?" I asked.

"No," Liz sighed. "Are you crazy?" Then she tilted her head and added, "Hmmm . . . do you think I need one?"

After an hour-long discussion about safety issues in a remote area, we decided she needed both a gun and a security system. While coming to this decision, Dorothy shared a story involving another lake house near hers.

Evidently, someone on the lake had been involved in a serious crime, and others wanted revenge. Questionable persons had stormed a cottage near Dorothy's and murdered a sleeping couple in their bedroom. They had disposed of the bodies in the lake, but it turned out to be even worse. The murderers had the wrong address. Those two innocent people died for something they had nothing to do with. Sadly, it didn't change the fact that they were dead, and their families were devastated. Hearing that story cinched our decision about a gun. We left right then. Piling into Katherine's SUV, we headed out for pawn shops, as her husband, Keith, had advised they would be the best place to start. On our way out of the drive, I suggested, being the designer, "If we're going to buy a gun, I think it should be pretty. I had a client once who had the daintiest little pistol with a tortoise-shell handle. It was lovely, and she proudly displayed it in a living-room cabinet."

Liz liked my idea, so we entered the first store asking to see pretty guns with tortoise-shell handles. Being a good ol' boy, the man behind the counter said, "Ladies, I ain't never seen that kind of a handle on a gun. But there's another pawn shop a couple of miles down the way that's much bigger than my place. He might have something you like." He spit a wad of chew into the bottle he carried at his side. "But before you leave, can I take a picture of you ladies? My ol' lady ain't never gonna believe this."

We shrugged our shoulders as he continued, "Most folks come in looking for a specific caliber or name brand. You know . . . a 22 or a 38. I never had nobody start their search asking for a pretty pistol. Like I said, my ol' lady ain't gonna believe this. But if I can show her a picture of y'all dressed up in all that finery . . . well, she'll believe."

We obliged the owner and then headed out for the next pawn shop. On the way, Katherine called her husband again. Now we knew the questions to ask about make and caliber, and we were good to go. We never did find a gun with a tortoise-shelled handle, but we located a 38-caliber Lady Wesson with a box of bullets thrown in. After a quick tutorial on loading and shooting, we went to lunch.

We returned to the lake house and saw that the security company was just leaving. That night we would have all slept more soundly if we had any idea of how to cut on the alarm. But our new purchase was loaded and resting in the top drawer of Liz's nightstand. That alone ensured that not a single one of us went near her room unannounced ever again.

We decided to have firing practice the next morning, so we pushed an empty oil drum over to the boathouse patio to serve as our target. We laughed, thinking about any person that might try to break in. Hopefully, he or she would have a lot of girth. That way, maybe we couldn't miss.

I was voted to shoot at the drum first. I had never even held a gun, but I was confident. So I held that piece of metal straight out in front of me and pulled the trigger. And fired straight up in the air. Everyone else ducked. I hadn't known about the kick from a 38, and when the kick naturally happened, my arm jerked toward the sky. Liz was laughing when I turned around. "If he's on the ceiling, you've got him!"

As everyone took their turn, the only thing we knew for sure was that the ceiling in Liz's bedroom would look like Swiss cheese. None of us could shoot that stupid gun, and the oil drum was safe.

Liz shook her head in defeat. "Guess it'll just be a deterrent unless I can scare him to death. Of course, I can always hope it ricochets from the ceiling to wherever the perpetrator is standing."

We fully intended to sign up at a local shooting range, but it would have to wait until our next trip. Things were about to take a turn for the worse.

The Unplanned Trip

After Tom and the children returned to Atlanta that night, we planned to simply relax for a few days together. We sat by the lake and shared our thankfulness for the gift of friendship we enjoyed. More importantly, for seeing Liz settled and happy.

The group left Wednesday due to obligations in Atlanta, but I decided to stay with Liz until Sunday. Then, we'd return to Atlanta for various doctor's visits. However, Thursday night, Liz woke up in a great deal of pain and was having trouble breathing. I called Dr. Matthews in Atlanta, who called 911 for the squad to take her to a nearby hospital. The minute we arrived, the staff went to work. Her lungs were full of fluid.

Liz was rushed to a special treatment room. I held her hand and watched the gruesome amount of fluid being drained. After the procedure was completed, Liz was admitted for the night. Sitting in the hospital room, watching her sleep, I was so scared. I knew there would be important decisions to make. I loved Liz with all my heart, but this was too hard. It hurt too badly. How was I going to be able to see it through? Either Liz would go through more chemo, more draining, more tubes, and maybe beat this hideous disease and live, or she would go through the same exhausting procedures and die. That was the reality we were facing. Could I do this? Could I be everything Liz needed?

I knew what I wanted to do. I wanted to walk away. How was I going to be able to suffer through this with Liz? Honestly, I wasn't sure I could handle it and be the person she needed me to be. But I also knew in my heart that I had no choice. Whatever was going to happen was going to happen. There was absolutely nothing I could do about it except love Liz through it all and stay by her side. Furthermore, I knew she would do the same for me.

I didn't sleep much in the recliner that night, but when I opened my eyes, Liz was staring at me. She laughed and said, "Thank heavens you're awake. I need to make three or four phone calls, get some breakfast, and then I'm ready to go home. Will you tell them I want pancakes? They can't refuse a dying woman her last request!"

I burst into tears and cried, "Don't you ever say anything like that again!"

Liz held out her hand and said, "Come here. I'm

sorry. I didn't think about how hard this is for you. I won't ever say anything like that again . . . but you'd better come back with pancakes."

After finishing a plate full of pancakes, and finally being discharged, we walked over to the doctor's office. When they called us back, we both took seats in front of his large desk.

He began, "Liz, the fluid episode was very dangerous. If it happens again, you're to come to the hospital immediately." Then he turned to me and said, "Are you staying with Mrs. Moore tonight?"

"Yes, I am," I replied. "Is there anything special I need to do for her?"

"You just need to be aware that there could be a catastrophic event. If that should happen, call 911."

Liz began to ask him a couple of questions, and I butted in, "Excuse me? Could you define catastrophic event?"

He calmly said, "With the build-up of fluids, she could die."

Stunned by his bluntness, my tears began to pour. Reality is a hard thing to swallow.

Liz looked at me and then back at her doctor. "Don't mind her. I'll take her outside and slap her around a little. After that, she'll be okay." And then she just laughed and laughed. You see, Liz had decided that she would die living. Never would she live dying.

I now understood I was to take that journey with her, and from that moment on, we'd take those steps precisely the way Liz wanted to, even though I did check on her about forty times that night. But, thank the Lord, there was no catastrophic event.

Can I Go Too?

Liz's health seemed to stabilize over the next few weeks, and she and her daughters decided to take a trip to visit her cousin, Tracy, while she was still able. The two had become very close when their grandmother died. If I'm honest, I'll have to admit that it was nice to have two weeks without feeling responsible for Liz's care. By now, I was exhausted and could tell that Matt needed my attention. He had been understanding, but one just knows when we might be carrying someone else's issues a little too obsessively, without regard to our spouse's needs. It was as if I always had a private keyhole into Matt's every thought, so I suggested we take a few days together to visit some friends, Beth and Dan, who lived in Virginia.

Beth took me aside when we arrived and whispered, "The guys are playing golf Saturday. So I arranged for us to spend the day at a conference that the Christian Broadcasting Network (CBN) is having. She knew I loved watching *The 700 Club* and thought it would be a good diversion for me after hearing of Liz's condition.

She was right. The afternoon at that conference completely changed my life. I don't know whether it was because I was emotionally needy at the time or just desperate for a renewed sense of my relationship with Christ. Regardless, that time refreshed me in a way I would never forget. When a group of us prayed in a breakout session, I received a new understanding of the workings of the Holy Spirit. It was as if everything I had ever known about my faith went from a prop plane into a supersonic missile. My eyes had been opened to a whole new realm of trusting my Savior.

Realizing what had just happened in my life was the answer I had been praying for regarding Liz, I was convinced that God's word was truth and healing was possible. Liz was a thoroughly good person, but tackling the subject of a relationship with Christ might be difficult. There were times she could be such a private person. Although, if I were ever going to approach the subject, this time in her life was probably the best. Hope could be her mainstay with all she was going through and what she would still have to endure. So I prayed, "Father, please make a way."

• • •

Several weeks later, it was my turn to go back to the lake to be with Liz. One morning, she casually asked, "Jan, what's the deal with you and Jesus?"

That was the opening I needed, but I had to be careful. I didn't want to give more information than Liz was asking for. I explained that as a young girl, my grandmother had introduced me to Jesus, a close friend of hers. Then I experienced other times that helped me understand how much I needed Him in my life. I discovered that truth more each day in ways I never anticipated.

Liz laughed and said, "Thank goodness you're not one of those Jesus freaks!" Then, changing the subject, she said, "I'm ready for breakfast. Let's have spaghetti." Now, that may seem like a strange breakfast item, but Liz's taste buds changed daily during this stage of her illness, so we never questioned her cravings. We just made sure to stock her freezer and pantry with almost everything we could imagine.

Nothing else was said that week, but I knew a seed had been sown. Coincidentally, I had received a telephone call before heading out to the lake. A friend from my prayer group called to see if I wanted to attend a healing conference with them the following Sunday.

I returned to the lake the next weekend to spend a couple of nights with Liz. The weather turned out to be glorious after enduring a soaking rain every day that week in Atlanta. The sun was a welcome sight in a sky of azure blue with soft, white clouds seemingly strolling by sporadically. There was a soft breeze, and it was simply perfect for sitting out on the dock to enjoy the sun's warmth. Whoever had been at the lake house last, presumably one of Liz's girls, had put all the lawn chairs in the garage. As I looked up from the lake, Liz had begun to drag one of the chairs down to the dock before I realized her plan. She was still weak from the treatments and multiple medications. I rushed over to help.

This story may seem far-fetched if you're unfamiliar with Georgia's red clay. But as Liz held one arm of the heavy Adirondack chair and I held the other, we began to slide. The next thing I saw was Liz following the chair as it pulled away from our grip. After hitting a slick spot on the clay, she fell backward and actually beat the chair down the hill. Once I saw she wasn't hurt, I couldn't help but laugh.

Liz looked up, laughed with me, and said, "I'm taking this chair. Go get your own." So, helping her up, we got her chair to the dock and successfully got her in the seat. Then I went back and slowly brought the other chair down.

When we were both seated with glasses of lemonade, I brought up the subject of the healing conference. I told Liz I would have to leave early Sunday morning but truly hated leaving her alone. She was quiet for several minutes.

She finally asked, "Can I attend the conference with you?"

"That'd be a great idea!"

Nothing more was said on the matter, but she was packed and ready to go by Sunday.

The conference was being held in a high school auditorium in downtown Atlanta. Liz and I knew it would be crowded, so we headed to the venue as we drove into town. After stopping at a J Christopher's in the area for her sausage and eggs, we found the school and met the members of my prayer group at the front entrance. This group of women and I had been together for over ten years and prayed for each other through almost everything you could imagine. We'd sometimes laugh and say that if anyone ever left our prayer group, we'd have to kill them. We all knew way too much about each other's secrets.

Suzanne, Bobbi, and Donna were waiting, and within minutes, Julie, Tudi, Marion, and Janet came running up, complaining that parking was a night-mare. They all had been praying for Liz's healing daily and were thrilled that she came with me. As we entered the building, we noted the huge crowd and that lower-level seats were already full. I was concerned about Liz having to walk up several flights of steps to get to the higher, empty bleacher seats, but with our help, she made it up better than expected.

A young pastor gave a message on trust. He assured us that we could trust in Christ's plan for our lives, and he shared several instances when people had prayed for years, and healing had never come. But he then shared a silver lining of how other miracles had brought comfort to those in pain and their loved ones. He quoted scriptures from the Bible for all the healing miracles during Jesus's time on earth. He added that miracles were still possible if we believed the Easter message that Jesus had risen and was alive today.

He then shared stories of several healing miracles he had witnessed in the last few months. One had been his own father, who had been healed of a heart condition just weeks earlier. After his message, the pastor asked if anyone wanted to come down to the front of the stage for prayer. He explained that together we were going to pray for and expect miracles. I didn't even look in Liz's direction but sat and stared straight ahead. Inside, I was dying to know her private thoughts.

Several people in front of us stood and walked to the end of the aisle and down to the floor area in front. With that, Liz stood up and asked if I would go with her for prayer. When I stood, the rest of our group rose as well. We all carefully made our way down to the floor and over to the center stage area. I held Liz's arm, hoping it wasn't too much to simply make it that far, knowing her strength was already fading.

We all held Liz's hands or arms and prayed with the young pastor as he prayed for everyone gathered in search of healing. As he prayed, I watched a tear trickle down Liz's cheek. It was the first tear I had seen her shed during this whole nightmare of ovarian cancer. When the prayer time concluded, and we turned to return to our seats, Liz looked at me and laughed, "We're definitely going to see a miracle today! It's going to be me getting back up those steps!"

Two days later, Liz was back in the hospital, having more fluid drained from her lungs. That process was repeated for months. There was always another procedure, test, or medication, and we learned very quickly that one of us had to be with her whenever she was at the hospital. Her needs were great, and even though the hospital staff couldn't have been any more helpful, we understood other patients depended on them as well. So we gladly took turns being the extra set of hands during her care. It was a time of long days and longer nights. Nothing seemed to make a difference. Liz was always tired and seemed to grow weaker as we all continued to pray for that miracle.

One afternoon, Dorothy ran into the hospital room and announced, "I've got an idea."

When We Thought It Would Never Happen

When the five of us had been at Dorothy's lake house before cancer came into the picture, we had put Katherine in charge of buying stocks. Together we decided we needed real money investments. So, shortly after, we purchased the piece of art in Carmel, each of us began to contribute a certain monthly amount. We discussed the stocks we thought were viable, and Katherine would make the actual transactions. We had been doing this for several years and now had a pretty good nest egg. Our long-term dream was to eventually sell every single stock in order to take a trip to Europe. Every now and then, one of us would mention that we should be sure to see Rome, Paris, and by all means, Venice, but that's about as far as our dream had gone. Just a lot of talk.

But now, Dorothy and Sue had decided it was time to make our trip. I personally believed they were insane. Liz was in no condition to attempt traveling, and having her that far away from her doctors made no sense to me. But Liz thought it was a grand idea. Katherine and I held fast to our reservations but figured we could plan the trip. Of course, that didn't necessarily equate with taking the trip.

Having used a travel agent on earlier European trips, I was put in charge of making all the arrangements. Actually, it was an easy task because I knew this particular agent only needed the information on where we wanted to go. She would gather the reservations for guides, cars, and more. I only needed to take care of the flights.

After hearing her recommendations for visiting all the countries we had in mind and still keeping Liz's condition a top priority, we decided on a cruise. And with that information, it was time for me to arrange the flights. The cost of the trip was now beginning to exceed our fund balance, so we decided to use frequent-flyer miles for the booking. I called Delta. The agent told me that flights came out six months before the desired travel date, meaning we needed to book the tickets in exactly two days.

On the stroke of midnight of that second day, I called Delta again. With total confidence, I told the young man on the other end of the line that I needed five first-class frequent-flyer tickets and gave him the legs of the planned trip. First we wanted to fly into De Gaulle and have a long layover in Paris to take a quick tour of the hot spots in that city. We then wanted to fly out that night to Rome, where we would spend two days before boarding the cruise ship. Finally, we wanted a return flight from Athens to Atlanta.

It seemed simple to me until he politely announced, "Ma'am, that will never happen. There is no way to get five frequent-flyer flights, let alone first class, with that many legs."

I begged. "Well, can you try really hard? There are five of us taking this trip . . . one has ovarian cancer. We've got to do this soon. Please help us work this out."

There was silence on the line before he quietly said, "Miss Jordan, my sister died of ovarian cancer last year. We'll get these tickets."

At three-forty-five that morning, he had booked all five tickets. From then on, I no longer worried about taking Liz on this extended vacation. If that young man could pull off our flight miracle, the trip had to be God's will.

If I explained just how sick Liz was when we boarded the plane to Paris, you would have rightfully thought we were lunatics for attempting this adventure. But Liz had her pillow and her blanket, as well as her determination. To help you understand the dismal reality of what we were doing, we checked with the

U.S. Embassy to ensure we knew what to do if an American citizen died in a foreign country.

The day of our trip arrived and the five of us, even with a wheelchair and tons of medication for Liz, made it to our gate on time. On the plane, Dorothy and Sue sat together, Katherine and Liz sat together, and I sat beside a man with the worst body odor I had ever smelled. Not only that, it was an overnight flight, and when the seats reclined for sleeping, I felt as though I was in bed with a stranger. It got worse. The odor was foul enough, but his snoring in my ear sounded like a hurricane gale. Finally, I had hit my limit and made sweet Sue change seats with me, promising it would only be for an hour or two nap. After just thirty minutes, she pulled on my sleeve and made me trade back. It was a miserable flight, but Liz slept through it all.

When we landed in Paris and exited the plane, the other three were to go to the baggage carrousel and then meet Liz and me in the main terminal with the luggage. I was to use the wheelchair we brought to bring Liz and our smaller carry-ons, which I had placed on her lap. Afterward, we were to meet our driver, who was scheduled to take us on a six-hour sightseeing trip. Never having pushed a wheelchair before, I knew nothing about wheelchair etiquette. I steered Liz into the elevator with her knees and head facing the back wall. Then I walked around to make sure she was okay. She was not.

Explaining, Liz said, "You back a wheelchair into an elevator with the patient's face looking out the doors . . . so she doesn't feel claustrophobic!"

"You're lucky to be upright in the damn chair," I whispered. "My knees are killing me from trying to turn away from that awful snoring, so you'd better behave yourself." Thankfully, the doors opened, and we escaped from my first wheelchair misadventure. But, trust me, there were more to come.

We found the driver and loaded the van with all of our luggage. With her pillow and blanket, Liz took the bench seat in the back, laid down, and covered up. I sat in front with the driver, and the other three took the middle seats. Liz slept while the rest of us quickly ran to see Notre Dame, the Eiffel Tower, the Left Bank art fair, and a quick, one-hour tour of the Louvre. The driver stayed with Liz as she slept, and he had all of our cell numbers in case there was an emergency.

It was soon time to return to the airport, recheck the luggage, and prepare for our next leg to Rome. We had let Liz sleep some more at the gate, but now it was time to board the plane. She didn't look well at all, and we began to second-guess every minute of the trip. Landing in Rome, we checked into the hotel for our two days of exploration before the cruise along the coasts of France, Italy, and Greece. That first night was beyond stressful. I didn't sleep at all for checking on Liz. She was extremely pale and lacked even a tiny amount of energy.

I walked over, sat down on the edge of her bed and took her hand. "Liz, I think we should go home." Tears were clouding my eyes. "The girls can finish the trip, and you and I can go back to Atlanta now."

Her eyes flew wide open, and she gasped. "If you think that I'm going back with you . . . and that wheelchair, you're crazy!" She inhaled deeply and pronounced, "I'll be fine in the morning. Now go to sleep." I knew not to push. Liz had made up her mind, and that was that.

The next morning, we all dressed to begin the day trip. Our first stop was Saint Peter's. When the driver arrived, we loaded the wheelchair and Liz with her blanket and pillow. The primary place she couldn't wait to see was Saint Peter's in Rome.

Unloading the wheelchair, Liz took her seat, and I walked over to push. Now, most of our tour was on cobblestone streets, and poor Liz swore we were trying to loosen her teeth as the wheels of her chair violently bobbled up and down.

Once we got to Vatican City, the ride was more comfortable. I pushed her through Saint Peter's Cathedral, and we stopped at the Pieta. Just weeks before, someone had vandalized that historic statue by Michelangelo. We noted huge chunks of marble missing from the body of Jesus, and I could see that Liz was touched by the attempted destruction and the marks it had left. I knew she was thinking about the destruction taking place in her own body, but I said nothing.

Following our group, we maneuvered down corridors and hallways filled with artifacts and exquisite tapestries, some made entirely of delicate, golden threads. Finally, we ended up in the Sistine Chapel. There, we stood, even Liz, and looked up at the most beautiful artwork we had ever seen.

Liz looked over at me and smiled. "If Michelangelo laid on his back for years to paint this, I can stand up to look at it. Amazing."

As we left Saint Peter's that day, something miraculous began to happen. Liz became a new person. She seemed to fill with new energy, and her color brightened. Her breathing even normalized, and after we had a wonderful lunch of antipasto and pizza, we actually felt safe leaving the wheelchair with the driver when we toured the Coliseum.

Liz's cousin called her that afternoon. Tracy was just checking to see how she was feeling. Liz immediately proclaimed what all of us were thinking. "Tracy, I was healed at Saint Peter's! I feel great, and I'm so glad we made this trip!"

The miracle continued for the rest of our time in Rome. We never used the wheelchair again on the entire trip. Liz was her old self, and it was wonderful.

The only daily reminder of her battle was getting that crazy wig on her head and fixing it just the way she demanded before going out in public.

After two days of enjoying all the sites in Rome, we walked up the gangplank to our cruise ship. Liz was still feeling strong. As she put it, she felt like new money and was ready to see Venice. We spent several hours shopping on our first day and found a cute little boutique in St. Mark's square. Then we took a ride on a gondola, had dinner at Harry's bar, and listened to the dueling orchestras in St. Mark's square before heading back to the ship.

The next day was spent at sea, and we simply lounged by the pool. Though a little too cool for bathing suits, it was perfect for Pina Coladas and a good book. That night we had planned to have dinner at the ship's five-star restaurant and were looking forward to dressing up. It was the end of October, and the ship was festively decorated for Halloween. Knowing we would be on the cruise over October 31st, I had packed what I thought to be darling headbands, which I brought to the table to hand out at dinner. One had cat ears, one had floppy dog ears, and one was like a monkey, and so on. I laughed as each lady grabbed and fought over the different designs. Each headband was loaded with sequins and rhinestones and looked perfect with our cocktail attire. We laughed, dined, and had such a fun evening.

After dinner, when Liz was tired of being dressed

up for that long, she was ready to change into more comfortable clothes. As she stood to leave, she reached up to pull her headband off and hand it to Katherine, who had liked it better and had tried to steal it earlier. Unfortunately, as Liz removed the headband, her curly wig came off as well. Our waiter had just brought over warm napkins when the wig left her head, but in typical Liz style, she merely looked at him and said, "I'm just having a bad hair day!" We all laughed until we cried or wet our pants. Thank heavens, the restaurant lighting was low, and the chairs were black. Finally, we all decided to go change into more comfortable and dry attire.

The days seemed to fly by way too quickly as we enjoyed Monte Carlo, Marseille, and the other ports of call. Soon back in Atlanta, Liz's miraculous recovery continued unabated. Then, one night shortly after our return, I received a call from Tom.

"Jan, I need to ask you a question," he began. "Liz is convinced that she was healed at Saint Peter's. What do you think happened? I've never seen such a change in anyone."

"I guess we'll never know for sure," I replied. "But Liz's version works for me."

Water, Water, Everywhere
⤇⤆

After the Thanksgiving and Christmas holidays, especially with Liz still feeling energetic, we all relaxed about her cancer. Dorothy's son, Ken, was getting married at their lake house, and we had been appointed to decorate for the ceremony. The wedding took place in the spring, a beautiful time at the lake with the azaleas in full bloom, which could work beautifully for centerpieces. Liz's job was to make all of the bows, Sue and Dorothy were to ready the house, and we all brought lots of that damn silver from the earlier trip to re-polish and use for the reception. All was Southern décor personified, with satin and lace table coverings showcasing greenery and azalea blossoms. As Katherine and I stood back to admire our work, the bride and groom arrived.

Dorothy came rushing up. "Something's wrong!" She had tears in her eyes, which was not her norm.

She repeated, "Something is very wrong. My son is furious. His wife-to-be is sweating like a horse."

Being naïve, Katherine and I said in unison, "Don't worry. She's just excited." Then, as we turned to find the bride, I added, "We'll go see if she needs any help."

Knocking on the door, we heard Lisa slur the words, "Come in."

We entered and saw her standing in a slip that looked like she had just stepped out of a bath. She had bath cloths under each arm, her hair was wet all around her face, and she dropped beads of perspiration from her chin. Not seeming the least concerned about the sweating, Lisa said, "I need to get on my bridal suit." She looked around, adding, "I've got a hat with a veil somewhere. Do you two see any white shoes?"

Katherine rushed into the bathroom and came back with fresh hand towels. Within minutes, those towels were soaked, and the sweat continued to pour even as Lisa seemed oblivious to it all.

Katherine started back for more towels, and I caught her arm and whispered, "Find a damn beach towel! These hand towels aren't worth a toot."

"I think she's drunk," Katherine whispered back.

"I'm not sure you sweat like this when you're drunk," I said. "I think Lisa's sick."

About that time, Dorothy cracked the door and softly asked, "Is everything okay?"

I pushed her out and said, "We're working on it."

By this time, Lisa was standing in a puddle of water. Katherine was in the bathroom loading her arms with towels when she called out, "Jan, come in here!"

I ran inside, and Lisa followed. Katherine pointed and told her to go back to her puddle. Then, Katherine looked at me and said, "If she's sick, she's dying. You can't lose this much fluid and live."

There was another knock at the door, and the groom walked in. We stood there with every towel in sight, mopping Lisa's body. When Ken saw the commotion, he turned and left.

Lisa looked at me and said, "What's his problem?" We shrugged our shoulders.

The next knock at the door came from Liz. "Everybody is waiting! What is the problem in there? Frank is standing with the groom, waiting for the bride!" Then Liz's eyes took in the bride, the sweat, and the puddles. She walked over and stared into Lisa's eyes. "Lisa, what did you take?"

"Nothing. Hand me my suit," Lisa said as she staggered over to grab her outfit.

We held her steady, and she stepped into the skirt and put on the jacket. She tried to button it up but missed a few of the buttons. She slipped on her shoes that we had finally found and slapped the hat with a veil on her wet hair. Katherine did her best to freshen Lisa's makeup, and I re-buttoned the jacket.

How that bride stood through the service, I will

never know. I had a feeling that Frank cut the ceremony really short as he took in Lisa's condition. The bride and groom left the minute the ceremony was over.

Two weeks later, Lisa checked into a rehab center for the third time in two years. We never did figure out how Ken totally misread Lisa, but the sad part was that he loved her and was committed to seeing her through the addiction. All Dorothy worried about was the mess that might develop if Lisa were to get pregnant. Thankfully, she didn't, and their marriage ended after her fourth stint in rehab.

Back to the wedding. That night after we had everything cleaned up, the silver stacked in each of our cars, the floors mopped, and the washer stuffed with at least fifteen towels, the five of us decided to go to a hole-in-the-wall restaurant for crab legs. As we sat together, cracking the legs, with juice running down our arms, we couldn't help but laugh. It had been some kind of a day.

Dorothy had downed several glasses of wine and was tired to the point of being punchy. "Did y'all know we had a trailer on the lot before we built the lake house?" she asked. "And trust me," she continued. "A very bad trailer."

Then she leaned back in her seat and rolled her eyes. "Well, you know what? Frank and I had some wonderful times in that ugly trailer." She grinned and added, "We had a sign on the front door that read, "If the trailer's rockin', don't come knockin'.""

"Dorothy! Your husband is a preacher!" Liz teased.

Dorothy tapped Liz on the shoulder. "A preacher. Not a priest. Big difference . . . Believe me, he's not celibate." Then with a wicked smile, she added, "He's not celibate at all."

We spent that night at the lake house, and when I finally got into bed, I reflected on the day and our night out afterward. Liz was feeling just fine, Dorothy had made the best of a bad situation, Katherine had learned that people don't die even after losing a tremendous amount of fluid, Sue had heard more than she probably wanted to about Dorothy's sex life, and I had promised myself I had eaten my last crab leg. My hands and arms still smelled terrible. It took weeks for that horrible odor to leave my nose.

A Kickback Changes Everything

Things truly seemed almost normal with Liz in remission. Work with Jordan Designs was as busy as ever. At last count, we had thirty open projects, mainly medical, along with a few high-end homes to design. The stress was manageable, but only because I wasn't worried about Liz. She and Tom were taking weekend trips and seeing a lot of each other during the week. He had brought such a new perspective to her life, and it was fun to watch. Everything was going smoothly until it was time for a large installation at Westside hospital. The subs we were using did incredible work and kept busy hanging wall covering, painting, installing carpet, and supposedly adding mahogany crown molding, stair railings, and cabinetry. I received a call from the hospital early Saturday morning. No one with the woodwork and cabinetry had yet made an appearance.

I assured them the company was likely on its way and then frantically began making phone calls. But, unfortunately, the company was closed on Saturday. Feeling nervous, to say the least, I tried Phil, the foreman, on his cell.

He returned my call an hour later. "Jan?" he asked. "What is the deadline for this project?"

"This job has to be . . . do you hear me, Phil? Has to be completed by midnight on Sunday," I replied as calmly as possible. The administrative wing was to open first thing Monday morning.

Phil questioned, "Does Mr. Jackson know this?"

Now, Mr. Jackson was the owner of this fine company, and Phil hesitantly shared that he left for the Bahamas on Friday, and no installation had been scheduled. I leaned back in my chair in total disbelief. Harry Jackson and I had discussed this deadline on numerous occasions. My mind whirled as I thought back over the many jobs that his company and Jordan Designs had accomplished together. I also ruminated on the amount of money those jobs had put in Harry Jackson's pocket. I may have been more furious at some other point in life, but I couldn't remember when.

Then Phil confessed, "Jan, we're nowhere near ready to install anything on this project."

I hung up and dialed the hospital administrator with this news; it was one of the most painful professional calls I had ever made. Not only was I letting the hospital down, but there were other subs who couldn't do their jobs until cabinets were installed. About four crews of plumbers, electricians, and more were twiddling their thumbs, anticipating delivery of the millwork at any minute. Though everyone tried to be understanding, tension filled the air.

On Tuesday, Phil called me and asked if they could install on Thursday. I made numerous phone calls to re-coordinate this disaster, and all agreed to begin installation Thursday afternoon. By working through the night, all would be ready for the other crews to complete the project. I gave Phil one stipulation; I wanted Harry Jackson to meet me there at four o'clock.

Thursday rolled around, and I was waiting in the administrative suite at four.

Checking all the woodwork and cabinets, I was relieved to see they looked very nice and were ready to install. I could not have been nicer to Harry and told him I would have a check for him upon completion.

Saturday afternoon, I got a call that the entire installation was complete, and Harry asked if I could meet him there for the inspection. So I immediately drove to the hospital for the final walk-through. After carefully checking each piece of wood and every cabinet, I planned to share my feelings with Harry concerning his failure to live up to the contract. He and I both knew that with the busy days in the life of a hospital, delays of this kind were totally unacceptable and could definitely affect our design firm's considerations for future projects.

Harry was standing at the entrance to the administration area when I arrived, and he walked with me as I checked everything. Feeling satisfied, I handed him the check and nonchalantly asked about his time in the Bahamas.

He had the nerve to say, "It was just okay."

I shook my head. "That's too bad. I was hoping it had been a really nice trip. Because . . . I can guarantee you it was an expensive one. You've done the last job you'll ever do for Jordan Designs."

As I turned and walked away, I heard a sarcastic laugh.

A week later, Renee called me into her office. "Jan, do you know anything about this check?" she asked.

I looked at the check she held from Jackson Woodworking for two thousand dollars.

"I checked through their file repeatedly, and I don't see where they owe us any money," Renee explained.

"Just send it back. It's probably one of Jackson's many mistakes," I said. "Plus, we won't be doing any more work with them." As far as I was concerned, we were done.

A week later, Westside hospital's chief financial officer, Paul Wheeler, called and asked me to come by at my earliest convenience. So, on my way out the door, I stopped by Renee's office to see if there were any other financial concerns between Jordan Designs and Westside.

Clicking several keys, she checked her computer files. "No. All jobs are current. We're in good shape."

But somewhere in the back of my mind, while I drove to the hospital, that call didn't feel right. I reported to the front desk and was immediately escorted back to Paul's office.

He asked me to take a seat. "Jan, I received a report this morning from a hospital vendor that you have been taking kickbacks on some of your work for us."

Swallowing hard, I shook my head. I could not have been more dumbfounded, and I had no idea of what that accusation even meant.

Paul continued, "Obviously, we asked for evidence. But we got the strangest reply. According to this vendor's records, you returned the kickback check." Then he smiled and added, "Jan, I know how much work you do in this city. Especially medical work. I was certain you would never jeopardize your reputation over two thousand dollars."

My pulse began to return to normal. I explained that I knew who the vendor must be and shared my earlier conversation with Harry regarding the fiasco with the administrative suite. I added that I was sorry that something so petty and deceitful had taken up Paul's time.

He smiled again. "One good thing came out of this for sure. They won't be doing any of our work either. We paid them close to thirty-thousand dollars last year. Between the two of us, that was a very costly lie." He pulled a file from the corner of his desk and added, "We're starting three new projects over the next few months. They'll be yours if you want them."

Tears filled my eyes as I nodded. "We want them."

That night I met the girls for dinner and relayed the details of the day's story. Their responses showed me how devastating that two thousand dollars could have been. Katherine explained how rumors of that kind spread quickly through any type of financial firm, even her own accounting company. The word kickback had a tendency to stir up worries.

Liz, with her typical short fuse, said, "We oughta beat the shit out of him! Wonder who else he did this to? Maybe some who didn't send the checks back?"

She pounded her fist on the table. "Well, he'll never work at our hospital again, either. The little turd."

Sue started laughing. "Bet he'll rethink his part in all of this."

Then Dorothy said, "Wait a minute. Let's think this through. Jan, you were being looked after. Suppose Renee hadn't questioned the check? Just deposited it into your firm's account? Do you realize how everything about this would have turned out differently? His accusation of a kickback would have stood."

Everyone was silent, knowing Dorothy was right.

She continued, "I know how you always pray for your business. How many times you ask us to pray for Jordan Designs. Our prayers were answered the minute that check was returned."

On the way home after dinner, I began to sob. Probably the stress of the last two weeks, but I truly think it was just plain gratitude for God's mercy. Whatever, it was also thankfulness for Renee and her thoroughness and integrity. I thought more about Harry Jackson and actually started to feel sorry for him. Even though I had to agree. He really was a little turd.

• • •

In the coming days, the more I thought about the kickback nightmare, the more I could see how our business was changing. It seemed that all I did these days was apologize for contracted work that wasn't quite up to par. I don't believe anyone ever loved their work more than me, but now, it was just different. With everything going on in my personal life, I needed a change.

Matt and I had been wishfully thinking about retiring. He was weary of traveling and only wanted to occasionally consult from home. I was beginning to feel the same. I wanted more time with my children and now grandchildren.

I had a talk with my staff the following week. It's amazing how God's timing is perfect. Renee wanted to move away from the hustle and bustle of Atlanta and travel with her husband. Three of our hospital contracts wanted to hire their Jordan Design teams as in-house design departments. Valerie wanted to continue residential design by helping me with my two favorite clients and their numerous design requests. She could do the legwork for these projects and take on additional design work independently. She was also interested in working from home, as she had remarried and wanted a family.

. . .

Within four months, all were ready to make their moves. I closed the doors to Jordan Designs and sold the building. After fifteen years of a planned and busy professional life, I was free. I was still doing design in a limited capacity and on my terms, and it felt great. Now, I had the time to be more available for Liz's needs.

This is Ridiculous!!!

⌒⌒⌒

My cell rang a few weeks later. It was Liz.

"Jan, remember your story about the kickback? Well, it got me thinking. I'm wondering if there's a lead time on coffins. You know, when you pick out the stuff, you have to wait for it to be made, then transported . . . kind of like your woodwork with the hospitals. I'm not going to want a coffin just because it's available. I want to see what can be ordered and go ahead and take care of it."

I couldn't believe what I was hearing. "Liz, you're doing great. This is ridiculous. You do not need a coffin right now."

"It's not ridiculous, and I want to plan my funeral. I know what I want, and I'm not leaving it up to chance. My girls would have no idea where to begin. What are you doing tomorrow afternoon? I'd like your help with all this." Then she paused. "I'll probably be the first person in the whole wide world to have an interior designer plan the aesthetics of a funeral."

I could hear in her voice that she was as serious as a heart attack. Once she made up her mind, there was no changing it.

"I made an appointment for three o'clock tomorrow afternoon at Memorial Gardens . . . off of Johnsons-Ferry Road, and I need you with me. Can you meet me there, please?"

"If you're determined, I'll meet you. But I don't know how to plan a funeral," I assured.

Liz laughed and said, "You just deal with the aesthetics. We'll get the group to handle the words and music."

We hung up, and her words echoed in my thoughts. *Handle the aesthetics. What in the world were aesthetics at a funeral?* I would soon find out.

Tuesday afternoon, I met Liz at Memorial Gardens. I was told that the first order of business was to select a plot. We must have looked at fifty as the funeral director escorted us around the cemetery in a golf cart. The first was too sunny, the second looked barren, the third didn't feel right, the fourth seemed too windy, and the fifth was too low and didn't have a bench. And so, the next two hours went until Liz saw the bell tower on a hilltop.

It was a lovely plot with benches, and Liz thought

she would enjoy hearing the bells toll throughout the day. It was perfect. She asked the price, and we were both stunned at the expense. But she cackled and asked, "Do you ever put these on sale?"

The poor man looked stunned. "No, ma'am."

She looked at me and shrugged her shoulders. "Why not? I think it's exactly where I'd like to rest!" With that, she exited the golf cart and walked over to the plot. Then, turning to me, with her hands on her hips, she said, "Take my picture. This way, you'll have a before and after!"

I burst into tears and fussed, "This is not funny, Liz."

She kissed my cheek and apologized. "I'll be good."

Now that we had the plot, we went back to talk about caskets, the term the funeral director seemed to prefer over coffins. We entered a large room with a long row of caskets on display. Liz critiqued each one as we walked through the room.

Looking at the first, she shook her head. "The inside of this one looks like the top of a Valentine's box of candy! Look at these stupid ruffles! I wouldn't be caught dead in this."

I turned to the director, and there wasn't even a hint of a smile on his face, but Liz and I dissolved into hysterics. The following casket was high-gloss black. Liz shook her head. "Looks like a defective baby grand piano." Finally, she settled on a mahogany casket with a simple interior and brass hardware. "This one looks distinguished. Couldn't have that reputation in life, but I guess I can in death." She laughed again.

By now, my cheeks were soaked. This wasn't funny at all to me anymore. Pardon the pun, but it was deadly serious. My best friend and I were planning her last moments on this earth, and it was breaking my heart.

The director then took us into a room with large tables surrounding the walls, showcasing samples of bronze plaques and marble headstones. There was a card displaying all the font options for the engravings. He could see that I was still visibly upset and asked if I wanted a glass of water.

Liz laughed that throaty laugh of hers and said, "Don't worry about her anymore. With the bronze and marble, she's in her element." Then, she turned to me and said, "Okay, this decision is all yours. Pick me out some classy stuff."

By six o'clock, the aesthetic elements were complete. Liz asked for samples and photographs because we had planned dinner with the group, and she wanted their final approval.

Leaving the cemetery, I couldn't utter any of the words I really wanted to say. I wanted to remind Liz of the healing at Saint Peter's and that our time today was premature. I wanted to say that I thought her timing sucked, but I didn't say anything. I knew I would only begin to cry all over again if I even opened my mouth. And though I could tell she was hiding it well, I saw how difficult it had been for her. I wanted to wrap my arms around my dear friend and never mention this day again.

But the five of us were having dinner, and I knew it would be the topic of conversation. Liz would proudly display all her choices for a consensus of approval. As the two of us summed up the afternoon with our group, we all laughed, cried, and slowly ate our dinner, though none of us were hungry anymore.

To break through the heavy blanket of sadness, Liz asked for my phone and pulled up the picture of her standing beside the bell tower. Laughing, she assured me, "I bet I won't look as fat in the after shot." She threw her head back and laughed some more. "If I can lose ten pounds, we'll redo this picture!"

Phone lines were hot the next day. The four of us mulled over Liz's plans; it was a lot to digest in a short period of time. Then my phone rang from each of her girls, questioning why I had allowed their mother to do such a morbid thing. She was feeling fine, right? But then Tom called to thank me for going with Liz to make the arrangements. He also wanted to tell me that her latest PET scan wasn't good, even though she had not wanted us to know. Another round of chemo-therapy had been scheduled. And possibly another surgery for de-bulking any new tumors. I was not to say anything to Liz; she'd tell us in her own good time.

When I hung up, I felt like every ounce of air had been sucked out of my lungs. I wanted to call Liz but didn't want to betray Tom's trust. I wanted to call the others but wished I didn't even know. *Why burden them?*

Just then, my cell rang again. Looking at the screen, I saw it was Liz. I clicked on and said, "Hi, lady," as cheerfully as possible. "You doing okay?" I asked.

"Where are you?" she asked.

"On my way home from the final cleanout at the office," I replied.

"Can you meet me at Starbucks on Papermill?"

"Sure," I said and clicked off, even though I wanted to say no with every fiber of my being. I already knew what Liz had to say, and it would be unbearable to hear it from her. Everything Tom had told me was bad news, and if I felt that way, I couldn't imagine how Liz felt. Somehow, I knew this time was worse than before. Dammit.

My phone rang again. Liz laughed and said, "I forgot to tell you something. The new architectural group at the hospital was fired today. They came to their first meeting and left with their hats in their hands."

"What? I just heard that they had been hired. What happened?" I asked.

"Well, it seems they had not been privy to the fact that all the colors in the universe had changed. They had the nerve to call lemon . . . yellow! To them, the grape was only purple. And they had no clue that pink had been swallowed up by raspberry. Guess what? They hadn't brought a single sucker, not even a gumdrop. What a bunch of dummies! See you in a few." The line went dead.

Grass Skirts and Coconut Bras

❧

Matt and I had finished building what we hoped would be our retirement home on Bald Head Island off the North Carolina coast. After the five of us fully understood what Liz's next few months would entail, we decided to take one more trip before all hell broke loose. It would be good to get away in advance of the chemotherapy started and another possible surgery date was scheduled. Liz and I would drive to the island midweek with a car full of accessories for the new house. Sue, Dorothy, and Kathryn would fly in that weekend.

The long drive was actually nice except for the constant noise of tinkling glass, scraping metal, and cracking wood from the jostling of all the accessories stuffed in the car. Liz and I finally got used to it, much like background noise. We played music, talked, and ate the entire way to the island, where we would catch a ferry.

After unloading the car of china, crystal, linens, and more onto the ferry, I left Liz to guard my treasures and hurried to park the car in its designated space. Then, I ran back to the ferry. I made it just in time for us to board before it headed over to the island. Once we reached the landing, Liz and I were fortunate to find two young men to help carry the accessories and luggage to the tram, which would take us to the new cottage. Thankfully, the two also helped us carry all the stuff up the cottage steps.

Exhausted, we grabbed two glasses and a bottle of wine. After we placed the emptied glasses in the sink, we retired to our rooms. The two of us were ready for a good night's sleep.

The following day we unpacked linens to the closets, china and crystal to the kitchen, and accessories to empty spots throughout. We went to the island club for a seafood dinner that evening and back to the cottage to make up the other guestroom beds for the rest of our group.

The weather was horrible on Friday as a storm had settled on the island. Checking the weather report, it first passed east through Georgia on its way to the Carolinas. Unfortunately, that meant the plane carrying our friends was not on time, and they wouldn't arrive until late afternoon. Knowing it would be too dark for Liz and me to drive on unknown roads, I arranged for a driver to pick them up at the airport in Wilmington and bring them to the ferry. That gave Liz and me plenty of time to formulate a mischievous plan.

We would fix a pitcher of margaritas once we knew they were on the ferry. I had brought five grass skirts and coconut-shelled bras, along with a few leis to give a tropical welcome. We blew up several balloons and decorated the six-seater golf cart. Using what we had, I can't tell you how tacky it looked with old pieces of rope, a few ribbons, and some flamingo inner tubes. We even put a big, inflatable alligator across the back. The more ridiculous mess we added, the more we laughed. We placed the flamingo inner tubes on the windshield to look like sunglasses, which was clever if you didn't want to be able to see to drive.

Realizing the decorating was taking more time than planned, we knew we had to make the margaritas and leave to meet the ferry as soon as possible. So, grabbing the glasses, we pulled out. Only to pull back in to put on our costumes, get the pitcher and head back out again. We held onto our leis and grass skirts, with the coconut bras over our shirts, as we braced the howling wind.

Rushing to back out of the driveway, with limited space, I knocked the front fender off of the golf cart. Liz and I didn't give it a thought and just kept going.

We were running really late. By the time we reached the ferry, the rain had almost stopped, and the wind had died down. The boat was just pulling up to the dock, and the sight of Dorothy's, Sue's, and Katherine's expressions were priceless. They couldn't hide their embarrassment as we put leis around their necks and handed each a margarita. Now, to make sure you have the full picture, there was a golf cart with a fender missing, decorations hanging awry because of the wind, grass skirts too small for our rather large behinds, thankfully covered in jeans, coconut bras that might have fit a thirteen-year-old, and hairstyles and leis that had been shredded by the wind.

In truth, the other three didn't look impressive either. Unfortunately, the inside deck of the ferry was already full by the time they arrived, which meant they made the crossing on the outer decks with the wind, rain, and splashing of the surging waves.

"Whose idea was this trip?" Katherine asked as she sipped her margarita on the way to the cottage.

By now, we were all tickled and maybe a little tired. We dodged the fender as we pulled into the garage and ran inside. That night we laughed together as the three shared stories of the flight's turbulence. Apparently, one of the flight attendants lost her balance and ended up in Dorothy's lap. She'd juggled an entire tray of drinks to no avail, and the liquid from all five glasses ended up on poor Dorothy. Her soaked seatbelt remained fastened for the remainder of the flight as the attendant wiped and wiped nearly every part of Dorothy's body! There were no smiles, especially from my friends, as they left the plane rubbing their white knuckles. But they were mighty thankful to have touched down in one piece!

After catching up and enjoying a spaghetti dinner, we retired to the various beds for the night, knowing tomorrow had to be better. At least we were together.

Pleasant weather returned to the island the next day, and a shopping spree ensued. On previous trips with Matt, I had scouted the area and knew exactly where to take my friends. Sue was building a mountain house, so we focused on finding great buys on cute pieces of furniture to fill in the small areas in our decorating plan for her new abode.

The first thing we found was a darling stick table, perfect for beside a chair, and then an old butter churn that had been made into a lamp. Next, we saw a set of fish plates we thought would be fun for Dorothy. But at lunch, she shared a confession. "The four of you have been giving me fish stuff for the last five years." She paused as if to gain the strength to go on. "I have not wanted to say this because I don't want to hurt your feelings . . . but I do not want any more fish shit."

My eyes grew wide. As a minister's wife, Dorothy had never said a swear word in our presence that I could remember. So we figured she hated 'fish shit,' and we would no longer buy anything fish-related. We gave them to Sue instead, who seemed to like 'fish shit.'

Next, we found a charming little oak chest, just right for a nightstand, a large old, galvanized bucket to hold wood for the fireplace, and a lantern or two for her porch. Again, we had gone brain-dead. We were driving back to Georgia with five women and all of our luggage. How would we get all this furniture home? Where there's a will, there's a way! Thank heavens, I had a Volvo station wagon, which would hold more than we expected as long as everyone but the driver held their luggage on their lap. For the next seven hours, the car was pretty quiet. Liz was to start chemo on Wednesday, and that reality seemed to settle in as we drove toward Atlanta.

I Miss My Wife

After arriving safely in Atlanta and unloading the over-packed car, Dorothy asked if we could all have a time of prayer. Of course, asking about prayer was nothing new for Dorothy, but I had the strangest feeling listening to how she worded her request that she was genuinely anxious for the upcoming week. Her concern would prove to be justified.

Liz's oncologist believed a second surgery was necessary before beginning the chemotherapy. Regrettably, there was a slip during the de-bulking surgery that week and the scalpel nicked Liz's colon. We were all devastated when her surgeon came out visibly upset as he explained the seriousness of that complication.

The costly error led to more than we ever anticipated, and Liz was sent home with a catheter and a feeding tube. Even though we were assured that these things happened and sometimes were easily correctible, we couldn't help the heightened anxiety as each day brought increased infection and pain. As usual, Liz remained the brave trooper and never complained. The four of us learned nursing skills as never before. Going back to north Georgia was not an option with the tube, so we had already decided to take Liz to my apartment in Atlanta. We took turns flushing her tubes, changing her bandages, and performing other procedures I never dreamed I would be able to handle. But I learned a valuable lesson through it all. You can do the impossible when love is involved.

In the middle of all this, I had to return to Bald Head to complete a design project for the Conservancy on the island and leave my best friend. But, of course, I was leaving her in the very capable hands of the other three.

Arriving on the island, it was so good to see Matt standing at the ferry dock. I had really missed him and felt guilty about my excessive travel schedule. I could tell something was bothering him as he drove the golf cart to the house; Matt wasn't usually that quiet. I decided to wait to ask questions until I was settled in and unpacked.

Cuddling together in bed that night, I finally asked if he was okay.

"I'm fine. But do I understand that you plan on going back to Atlanta in two weeks?"

I tried to explain. "Liz had a serious complication from that surgery, and I need to be there."

"Jan, has it ever occurred to you that I have been alone more in the last year than in the entire time we've been married? Can't you get some of her family or your other friends to take more time with Liz's care?" He paused. "I miss my wife."

"You could come to Atlanta with me," I suggested as tears slipped down my cheeks.

"I could. You're right," Matt agreed. "But we didn't build this house so we could stay in Atlanta."

I knew he had a point, and this was not the first time I sensed his unhappiness with my times in Atlanta. But it was the first time he had voiced his thoughts. "Matt, the next two months will be critical for Liz. I don't know why, but I just feel that she needs . . . me."

I drew in a deep breath and continued. "Liz has her girls and Tom, but the four of us know she's happier and more comfortable with us doing the dirty work that accompanies her illness. We're all taking turns, but now that I'm retired, I have the most available time. I know it's difficult for you, but I can't let her down. If you'll bear with me during these next few months, her cousin will have finished her nursing degree and can help all summer."

Matt slowly smiled, but I needed to say more. "There's another issue we need to talk about. The lease on our apartment is up next month, and Liz cannot go back and forth from north Georgia. I know you'd like to give it up, but I would love to extend our lease on the apartment for one more year."

Matt's smile vanished. "I'll sleep on it," he said as he rolled onto his side facing the wall.

I awoke the next morning to the smells of coffee and bacon; Matt had made a delicious breakfast. I slipped on my robe and bedroom shoes and walked toward the kitchen.

He met me with a steaming cup of coffee. "Break-fast is served," he said with a smile. Then, sitting down, he took my hand and added, "I know how much you care for Liz. We'll extend the lease. We'll make it through the next few months, and you do what you need to do."

I sighed with relief. Matt had always supported every aspect of my life, professionally and personally. My time with Liz was no exception.

Then he offered, "I'll be there if you need me to help in any way."

. . .

Two weeks later, I returned to find Liz dealing with a mess. After having more tests, the doctor decided to push the chemo out a while longer. The nick in her colon was not healing. With that news, Liz seemed to give up.

All four of us were concerned that she had quit fighting, so Dorothy came up with a plan. We took Liz to a new store that had just opened, called The Scrapbooker. We bought two scrapbooks and at least one of every decorative page they had on the rack. We figured if we had a project, especially one that would take a long time, Liz would get excited. Once anyone gave her a project, you could bank on the fact that she would complete it.

Katherine and I went to the lake house in north Georgia and brought back all of Liz's photo albums and loose pictures, along with anything else we thought was small enough to use on a page and would rekindle a good memory. This could be a gift for her twins, a project many mothers believe they'll do in their later years, but we needed it to happen right away.

The dining room table in my apartment was cleared, and the scrapbooking began. Two weeks later, Liz was a different person. She was having a good time reliving each special event in her family's life. As Dorothy, Katherine, Sue, and Liz worked daily shifts on the collection, sometimes during the day and sometimes at night when sleep wouldn't come for Liz, I was the one sent back to the store with a list of needed supplies. I'll have to say the project was cathartic. We laughed as we saw her babies with food all over their faces, dogs jumping into the backyard pool, and birthday parties with tons of cute decorations. We cried when Liz reminisced over the pictures of her mother and daddy, her wedding to Bill, and a brother she had lost long ago.

Even with Liz's excitement, some days were better than others. But after three emotional weeks, the scrapbooks were complete. Her determination took over as she was reminded of life's journey with its ups and downs. If only her body had come alongside. The good days seemed to lessen, and the bad ones increased, but through it all, Liz remained steadfast.

After one afternoon nap, Liz walked out of the bedroom with a huge smile. She had just phoned her oncologist and had invited him to dinner. Now, I was not a cook, but Dorothy was there, and she was. She and Liz planned the menu, and I left for the grocery store. Sue and Katherine were called and told to come for dinner at six and to bring the wine.

That night we all enjoyed a lasagna dinner. Dr. Matthews, though tired, seemed to pep up with our attention, and, bless his heart, he shared story after story of ovarian cancer survivors. By the time he left, we had all benefitted from an injection of hope, including Liz. It was as if the atmosphere in that apartment experienced a rebirth. Excitement was in the air. We knew that miracles were indeed possible, and a new sense of expectation permeated deeply in our hearts. That night, one of those miracles was claimed for Liz. I went to bed praying only two words. *Please, Lord.*

The next few months brought little change. I would go back and forth to Bald Head, Sue would go back to the mountains to check on things there, Dorothy would have church projects and meetings, and Katherine still had her young children to care for, but Tom was wonderful. And Liz's girls would also take turns being with their mother. With our combined shifts, it all worked out, and Liz always had a care-giver. But, one of the things Liz enjoyed the most was when she and Tom spent the weekends at his compa-ny's lake house in north Georgia.

However, as winter approached, Liz endured one bad report after another. The colon issue had now caused an opening to appear in her stomach. It seemed like anything that could go wrong did, and we could do nothing for our friend but love her and pray.

Yet, even with the decline, Liz didn't lose her sense of humor. We could watch her food pass through the feeding tube. She'd laugh as she watched a strawberry, then a blueberry, and then another strawberry slide through the tube. "Bet you'd never thought you'd see a fruit salad in such a disgusting manner!" But, oddly, it wasn't disgusting at all. We were thankful she was getting nourishment and at least some vitamins were giving her a little more stamina.

Late one afternoon, when we were all sitting around and finally sewing lace on the towels we had bought years ago, Liz announced she had a plan. She called it her 'dying plan.' She had decided she would live seven more days, no more and no less, and she had written down exactly how it would go.

Her first step, already taken that day, was to call the DeKalb County Coroner. She asked how they picked up dead bodies, and he politely asked in return, "Ma'am, can you tell me whose body we'll be picking up?"

He wasn't quite prepared for her answer. "Mine," she said. Then she asked if he could assure her he wouldn't use any sirens; she didn't want to bother the other residents in the apartment complex. She even asked if she could make a reservation seven days from the call. I know the Coroner hung up thinking her call had to be a sick prank.

Explaining the rest of her plan, most would have thought she had no idea of what she was saying. Anyway, who can plan to die in an exact number of days? But, Liz was far different than anyone I had ever known, and her plan scared me. I knew that she had a will of iron and we had to find a diversion.

The four of us decided to take her back to north Georgia for a week at the lake. By this time, it took a second car with no passengers, to take all that was needed for Liz's care. But it was worth every minute of the panic and packing. We had a wonderful week at the lake and derailed her crazy, seven-day plan.

When Liz was napping, Sue had brought hundreds of scripture cards, and we each wrote notes on the backs of the cards. We placed them all into separate envelopes with a date on the front and Liz had enough for an entire year, opening one each day. I remember finding the remainder of those cards months later and counting that fifty-six were left.

While enjoying our time at the lake, Liz called me into her bedroom. "Okay, Miss Designer. We're going to pick out my outfits for the funeral." Several months before she got sick again, Liz had purchased a stunning black Saint John's jacket and slacks and another Saint John's outfit in purple. The second one still held its tags. "I spent a fortune on these two outfits, and I'm going to wear them!"

I tried to force a smile and she continued. "I was thinking . . . the purple would look perfect for the viewing. It's more cheerful. But then, I want my clothes changed so that I am buried in the black. I'd like the purple set given to my cousin . . . with her sorry husband, she'd never be able to afford something like this."

"I want to have on earrings. You can use some of my gold ones. The black will need my gold and diamond choker and the matching bracelet. And make sure I'm wearing all my rings with both outfits. Then right before they close the casket, to go to the cemetery. I want all the jewelry removed and given to my girls. Don't put any shoes on me. Nobody sees them anyway, and my feet have been hurting like crazy. Just some warm socks because my feet stay cold."

Tears flooded her eyes. "There's something else I want to be put in the casket. I want a picture of the five of us. Just hide it where I'll know where to find it . . . maybe in one of the pockets in the black suit."

I gave her a hug as my eyes poured. "You're killing me."

That was one of the longest days of my life, but I remembered later that she had called me back and told me exactly which picture she wanted. She was so bossy, but I can't even tell you how much I loved that woman.

The Difficult Conversation

The four of us watched as our friend went through the final stages of this horrible disease. We could do nothing but make sure she was comfortable and cared for. Liz was determined not to leave this world without doing everything she could for everyone she knew. We had hired a nurse a few weeks earlier to be with Liz when we couldn't. Her name was Ellen, and she was an incredibly jovial person. More than once, when Liz was feeling poorly and Ellen was a bit too happy, I'd see Liz roll her eyes. But through what must have been long conversations in the middle of the night, Liz had learned that Ellen was virtually homeless. Her husband had died several years before, and her son could not hold a job for longer than a few months. Helping him had depleted Ellen's savings.

Liz was on the phone the following day with a personal friend who worked for social services. Two weeks later, housing had been secured for Ellen and her son. It was a one-bedroom apartment, but the living room was large enough for a good-sized sofa bed. Liz had sent a check to cover all of the estimated expenses for an entire year.

Then I received a phone call. "Jan, I need you back in Atlanta a.s.a.p." It was Liz.

"Are you okay?" was my first question. Apparently, Liz had forgotten that I was flying in the very next day. It was obvious that her pain meds kept her foggy, although they really did help ease the pain.

Arriving on Saturday, as initially planned, she gave me my marching orders. When we had first moved Liz to the north Georgia lake house, all sorts of things from her Atlanta home were put into storage. She handed me the key to the unit and said, "Clean it out. Make Ellen's new apartment decorator-friendly. Whatever you need that you think is important, put it on my credit card." She opened her purse, pulled out her wallet, and gave me her card.

Matt and I followed a truck to Ellen's new place a week later. By the time we placed everything from the storage unit, I only needed to buy a lamp, one end table, and a sofa bed. We even had silk floral arrangements in boxes that added nice color and brightened up the rather dreary gray-painted walls. Accessories were placed, art was hung, and Liz had two window cornices in a bright floral, perfect for the living room. Finally, I unpacked two new drapery panels that worked nicely in the bedroom.

The only thing left from the storage unit was a large box of Bill's tools that he had promised to pick up for over a year. I figured that because he had never come to get them, he didn't want them. Therefore, when I saw another resident pulling into a parking space near Ellen's place, I asked if he needed any tools. He was thrilled and loaded them into his truck.

Liz called me the next morning. "Did you see any tools in the storage unit?" she asked. "Bill's name was on the rental agreement, along with mine, and they called him to make sure it was okay to release it for rent, now that it was emptied. So he wants to come to get the tools."

Not wanting to upset Liz, I said, "No problem. I'll get them and take them over to his place."

Matt and I quickly drove over to Ellen's apartment, but the truck with the man was no longer there. Knocking on a door, a lady answered; she didn't know anybody with a truck. Checking every apartment, we couldn't find a soul that knew any gentleman with a bright red truck. The only thing we could figure is that it may have been the maintenance man for the complex, so we called the office of social services. We finally located the director of maintenance and explained our predicament. He promised to get right back to us as soon as he checked with the crew for that area.

When he called back, he said he had located the red truck, but unfortunately, the tools had already been sold. *How was I going to tell Liz?* I decided to take a different approach and called Bill.

When he answered, I began to explain, and thankfully, he started to laugh. "Jan, I didn't want the tools back. I was just coming to get them out of Liz's way. I didn't want her to have to worry about them . . . how's she doing?"

"She's incredible, Bill. But we're just taking it one day at a time."

There was a long pause, and then he asked, "Do you think it would be okay if I came by for a short visit? I'd like to see her."

Thinking back to the scrapbook and all those tears and good memories, I said, "I think she'd like that."

Bill visited Liz once each week after that. Sometimes he took flowers or her favorite caramels from a little bakery near their old house. There were times when Bill and Tom would be there with her together. It was good medicine for all of us to laugh and share our Liz stories, and the visits were such good encouragement for her girls.

One night after everyone had left, and it was just Liz and me, she began to softly cry. "Isn't it wonderful how God has brought everyone in my life back to tell me goodbye?"

I could only nod.

Then she asked a question, one I had hoped she would voice for so long. "Jan, how do you know there's a heaven?"

"Liz, do you believe the Bible?" I asked.

"For the most part."

"Why don't we spend this week studying the word 'heaven:'" I suggested. "I've got some books I think you'll enjoy, and we'll investigate what the Bible has to say about heaven."

That week was an answer to prayer. We read Randy Alcorn's book, *Heaven.* Then we read a few additional books about people with near-death experiences who described what they saw, and we related their stories to what the Bible said about heaven. The discussion that had the most influence on Liz's final decision about whether or not heaven was real was about a little boy. He had become very sick and told of going to heaven and returning to tell his parents what he saw. The part that sealed it for Liz was the little boy describing Jesus and talking about the 'markers' on his hands. She knew a three-year-old wouldn't know about the nail-scarred hands. She was convinced he had seen Jesus.

When we finished the last of the scriptures, Liz asked, "How do I know I'll go there?"

"It's very easy," I replied. "You just repent and ask to accept Jesus as your savior."

She related a time from years ago when she was a young girl, and she had done precisely that. But then, with tears, she asked, "Can I do it again?"

As hard as it was, Liz got out of her bed and knelt with me on the carpet as we both rededicated our lives to Jesus with the words, "Jesus, I believe you died for me and rose again. I admit I am a sinner, and I need your love and forgiveness. Come into my life, forgive my sins, and give me eternal life. I confess you as my Lord. Thank you for my salvation. Amen."

That was the last time Liz ever got out of bed. But she was content, and there was no doubt in her mind, or mine, that she would enter those pearly gates.

As we studied, stories of the Apostle Peter were Liz's favorite, which was most understandable. He was a take-charge person, occasionally putting his foot in his mouth, and was about as determined as anyone I had read about. Peter's personality lined up with Liz's to a tee. But she had trouble remembering his name due to the effects of all her medications. One of the last words she ever spoke to me was, "Help me one more time. What's his name? The one I'm supposed to look up when I get to heaven?"

I would always repeat, "Peter. His name is Peter. And he's going to love you, and you'll love him!" I answered her question with the understanding that we may not have had the miracle we asked for, but we had a much bigger prayer answered. A miracle for eternity.

Two days after that last question, I said goodbye to my friend as she closed her eyes for the last time and slipped away. That night I had a dream, a cherished gift from God. I saw Liz standing on the landing of a huge stairway in front of a tall, stained-glass window. A light projected the colors of the window onto her form, and she looked radiant as she threw me a kiss.

Even with the passing of time, I still picture Liz asking Peter, "When is Jan coming? We've got so much to do. That group needs to hurry."

Just Following Orders

After the four of us had reconciled ourselves with the fact that Liz was no longer with us, we knew her funeral needed to be organized. Somehow we pulled ourselves together and got into party mode as Liz had specifically instructed in her written plan.

Number one stated that not one of us was to speak at the actual service. She wrote that her funeral was not to be a tear fest; we were to be as cheerful as possible, knowing she was with Peter and no longer in pain. Number two listed her pallbearer preferences- Matt, Keith, Frank, Tom, and two nephews, Chip and Todd. Number three read that her daughters were to do her hair and makeup if they were able. If not, Liz listed the name and phone number of her hairdresser. Next, there was to be a viewing the evening before the funeral. But she wanted it referred to as a party. A classy celebration of life party. There was to be plenty of Kendall Jackson Reserve red and white wine, several varieties of cheeses and crackers on our silver trays, and fruit trays of melons and berries. A video should run of only good photos, no bad ones. She noted that the twins and her cousin could handle that responsibility. Finally, she wrote that she wanted to copy Sue's service for Lilly with the bagpipes. She had even added a note with a smiley face for us to check if there was any truth to the legend that they wore nothing under the kilts. They were to play *Amazing Grace*, and she also wanted a vocalist to sing *Ave Maria*.

Reading that request, Sue said, "I didn't know she was Catholic!"

I laughed and said, "Don't ask questions. We just need to follow Liz's orders."

We could not forget that the purple Saint John's outfit was for the viewing, and the black one was for the funeral. Following that, her next command was to make sure her funeral was as nice as Lilly's. She wasn't about to take second fiddle to a three-pound dog. Finally, if she had forgotten anything, we should do whatever we thought was best. As long as it was classy.

The day of the viewing was more like a circus. Katherine was in charge of the food and wine, and Sue and Dorothy were to set up and run the video and make sure that calls extending private invitations were made to everyone named on Liz's list. My duty, besides overseeing that everything was beautifully decorated, was to get the purple and black outfits with the matching jewelry and without any shoes, just warm socks. I thought back to all the times we had to help Liz walk due to the neuropathy that plagued her feet. No shoes would be good.

The viewing turned out to be a party Liz would have thoroughly enjoyed. Most everyone present shared at least two or three Liz stories, which included several the four of us had never heard before. But the central themes were always typical Liz, and their words added love and humor to the evening of memories. At one point, toward the end, I almost thought of walking into the private viewing room. Everyone had said how beautiful Liz was, but I had decided that was a step I was unwilling to make. My memories of Liz were so vivid, and that's just the way I wanted to leave them. I wanted to remember her laughing and telling jokes, trying on lingerie, and being her crazy self.

After the last person left, the other three went in for their personal goodbyes while I gathered trays and leftover wine. Mindlessly caring for this task, I pictured Liz scolding Peter for his infamous denials and the rooster crows. I remembered how that story bothered her and was sure she would bring it up, probably at their first meeting. I couldn't help but smile as I took the video and unopened wine to my car.

. . .

Thankfully the weather was lovely the next morning. After the viewing, Dorothy and Frank had spent the night with Matt and me at our apartment. We spent a few hours together, both laughing and crying over the memories of the last twelve years. Then, we dressed and left for the eleven o'clock funeral around nine-thirty. I had promised Liz that I would not to be late and would make sure everything looked flawless.

It did. The spray of greenery and red roses was gorgeous. Liz had asked for donations to go to several of her favorite charities in lieu of flowers, but the four of us had sent bouquets of red roses to encircle the head and foot of the casket. We were grateful to be relieved of any speaking duty; none of us could have made it through a speech. The moment was too tender. After a few other friends spoke, a long trail of cars was directed to the burial site. The bagpipers were already there, and the melodies from their pipes could not have been more stirring. But the woman who sang *Ave Maria* was the worst I had ever heard. Honestly, she didn't even come close to hitting those incredibly high notes. And I didn't dare look at Katherine, Dorothy, or Sue; we would have burst out laughing. I could just hear Liz saying, "Who in the hell chose her?" What made it worse was that the singer actually brought an old-fashioned record player for her soundtrack. We later learned that the funeral director had run six extension cords for it to power up. The record was so scratchy we even doubted if the arm had a needle.

After Frank shared some of the most heart-warming words I had heard describing eternity and the joys we can expect, all stood to leave. Somehow it seemed as if our four pairs of feet wouldn't budge; the thought of walking away was too final. A finality we weren't ready for.

Telling the husbands goodbye and that we'd catch up with them a little later, the four of us walked over to the benches nearby. No one said a word as we sat and stared at Liz's gravesite. We watched the workers lowering the casket into the ground. Finally, the funeral director came over and asked if he could do anything more for us. I'm fairly sure he wanted us to leave as the men pushed the remaining dirt into the grave.

But we weren't ready to leave Liz; we just watched as if it were some sort of movie playing out on a stage that might have a better ending. You see, we knew in our hearts that this story of Liz would never have an ending, and she would be with us forever in our memories. Comforting thoughts we could bring forth at a moment's notice. We just sat there, each in our own personal grief. We shared occasional tears, and then another voiced memory would bring shared laughter. The cycle would then move to a deafening silence as we sat glued to the benches. I had hoped for one of those times when you might pray to wake up from a bad dream and experience the relief that it wasn't real. That relief never came. Liz was gone, and we had to learn to live with the pain. Hours later, as daylight was beginning to fade, we slowly stood and walked to Sue's car. But now, it was just the four of us.

Understanding the Reality of Grief

Days passed, and somehow I couldn't get everything back together. I wondered if I even made any sense on phone calls. My body was there, but the part of me that had always been able to function through any crisis had been buried with Liz. It all seemed so strange. I had lived for over thirty years without even knowing this woman, and now the void of her was a piece of my life that I was missing. It was as if all my tears had washed it away. I didn't want to go anywhere, I didn't want to be on the phone, and I honestly didn't want to be at home. I didn't want to talk about anything; I only wanted silence and seclusion to relive every moment. There was much I felt I hadn't said to Liz, so much more I wanted to do with her, and yet so much I wanted to forget. The nights she cried in my arms, the days spent helping her fight the pain, the horror of those final medical reports, and the depth of frustration when the sad truth of those last days was unmistakable.

I spent the next few weeks just sitting in my car, not wanting life to interrupt my solitude. We had all prayed so fervently; we took communion regularly. It's hard to trust with all your heart when the expected miracle never comes. I can't imagine how many other people were asking the same question I was about their loved ones. *Why?* I didn't hear from Katherine, Dorothy, or Sue during this raw time of grief, and I wasn't surprised. They were dealing with this same trauma in their own way.

Eventually, I received a note from Sue. With all the sincerity of her heart, she had written, "This is worse than losing Lilly." In return, I could hear Liz's thoughts: "She better miss me more than that spoiled three-pound dog!" I have to admit that Liz's imagined response brought a smile.

After another month of wallowing in grief, I had an idea. I made three phone calls and scheduled a dinner. I didn't want to face any more days of this horrible sadness by myself and felt the four of us needed to meet and spend an evening discussing all the happy times. We needed to shake off the bad and put on the good. Even if it came with buckets of tears. Somehow, after knowing that I would soon see my friends, I started feeling better. But, I wondered if it was a false sense of well-being. Would being together only revive the pain? Who knew? We'd just have to see.

I arrived at Houlihan's that weekend about ten minutes before our agreed-upon time and asked for a booth tucked in the back. As each of us arrived and our eyes met, tears fell without a word. Sue was the last to walk in, and we waved to get her attention. She rushed back and gave us each a hug, and sat down. "Jan, I'm so glad you planned this tonight. I've missed you all so badly. I just can't quit thinking about Liz; I want to talk about the happy times. I want to relive all of the crazy things we did, all of the laughs . . . I don't want to be sad anymore. I want to remember that big laugh of hers. I want to get all the tubes, surgeries, and disappointments out of my mind." She wiped a tear from her cheek.

Dorothy confessed, "And I want to stop questioning God as to why Liz wasn't healed. I want to remember how He gave us extra time after Saint Peter's. How He let us make so many more memories with her. I really do want to be thankful."

Katherine agreed. "I want to remember all of our trips."

With that statement, I had an idea. "Ladies, we need to take another trip," I began. "But it needs to be someplace we've never been before. A place where we won't drown in old memories. Somewhere we can start new memories . . . and enjoy the old ones."

Dorothy raised her hand. "We have just bought a

time-share in Cabo in a gorgeous part of Mexico. That would be a good place for us to start over." She stopped herself. "Let me rephrase that. A place for us to continue. I don't want to start over. We can take Liz with us in all the good memories . . . as we make new ones."

We all agreed and brought up the calendars on our cells. The date was set for the third week in February. The four of us had something to look forward to. Something that was desperately needed by all.

No Shoot!

Rushing into our terminal gate, I saw the other three pacing. "It's time to board!" Katherine yelled in my direction.

"I know, but I had to change cars with Matt before I left," I explained as I rolled my eyes.

We had booked first class with our miles, and in minutes, were comfortably sipping glasses of chardonnay in the spacious seats. There was no immediate conversation; we were all lost in our own thoughts. But I could see by the expressions that once in a while there were smiles in our hearts, secret smiles we held so dearly, some memories we shared, and some private. I glanced across the aisle at Dorothy and Sue and noted their tears as I wiped my eyes. Wouldn't you know that there was an empty seat in the first-class cabin directly in front of Katherine? It reminded me of watching President Kennedy's funeral long ago; I'll never forget when the horse passed by without a rider. Somehow, I felt the empty seat was the same sort of tribute to Liz.

Suddenly, Dorothy turned toward me in total disbelief. "They are taking our luggage off of this plane!" Then, she looked out the window again and added, "Oh my gosh, they're replacing our bags with golf clubs!"

I hit the bell for the flight attendant. When she finally came to our seats, we explained what Dorothy had just seen and demanded as kindly as possible for them to get our bags put back on the plane. The attendant explained that the aircraft was over the weight limit, and unfortunately, our bags were the heaviest items they had loaded. Apparently, the golf bags weighed less, and the staff would mark our suitcases top priority on the next flight to Cabo. As hard as she tried, her logic failed to sound convincing. Having husbands that traveled to play golf in resort areas quite often, there was no doubt in our minds that the airline preferred complaints from a few women over the possibility of losing corporate accounts. The four of us began laughing at the same time. "Where's Liz when we need her?" Sue asked. "She would've gotten our bags on this plane."

After the plane landed safely, we stepped into the humid climate of Cabo. Having had several glasses of wine, our suitcases no longer seemed such a big deal. We had endured lost luggage before and had wisely packed clean underwear, medications, and makeup in our carry-ons. We felt sure the hotel had a gift shop that could handle anything else we needed. After completing all the paperwork at the front desk for the late-arriving luggage, we stepped out of the terminal to hail a cab.

Dorothy sat up front with directions in hand, but our poor driver didn't speak Southern and couldn't understand a word she said. Not only that, his driving left much to be desired in that he seemed highly nervous but still chose to drive over every single posted speed limit. After whispering our concerns to each other in the back seat, Katherine finally tapped the driver on the shoulder, prepared to ask him to slow down. Before she even got a word out, he threw both hands up and yelled, "No shoot!"

Stunned, we looked at one another as Dorothy explained that we had no gun. We simply wanted him to slow down. We could see that he was visibly shaking, and Dorothy bravely asked, "Are you okay?"

In broken English, he explained that he had been robbed earlier that day and couldn't calm down. Still trembling, he told us he had no money and again pleaded for us not to shoot him.

Dorothy assured him that we were friendly and motioned for the rest of us to shut up and sit still. She entertained him for the rest of the drive by talking about the charming scenery and listening to every detail about his family and where they all lived.

Finally, as we pulled into the resort, we breathed a combined sigh of relief. He drove up to the Number Three unit, our condo for the week, and we each tipped him nicely as we said goodbye and wished him a much better and safer day. He was still nodding in agreement as he drove away.

Though our condo was on the second floor, having no luggage made it an easy climb. The manager had mailed Dorothy a key, but as luck would have it, it didn't fit the lock. We followed each other back down the stairs and walked what seemed to be a mile to the front office. Stepping inside, Dorothy explained our situation with the key. The woman behind the desk couldn't have been more friendly and accommodating as she opened a cabinet and handed Dorothy a bright new shiny key to Condo Three. Laughing, she said how sorry she was about our inconvenience, but with several recent robberies, the staff had just changed all of the locks. For some reason, she felt it essential to add that no one was killed or injured by the intruders, and she was very thankful.

After hearing that news flash, the poor taxi driver seemed calm compared to the four of us. Walking back to our unit, we rehashed the local news and the happy ending that no one was killed. I couldn't help but laugh when I said, "The intruders are going to be sorely disappointed if they try anything on us. Without suitcases there's nothing for them to loot!"

Just then, Sue freaked. She had left her carry-on

bag in the cab. We had no idea of the taxi company's or the driver's names but rushed back to the office to ask for help. As we neared the building, a cab was driving away, and sitting on the reception desk was Sue's bag. The clerk asked Sue to check and confirm that everything was accounted for and then commented on the driver's kind words and compliments for the nice ladies he had dropped off there. Apparently, he only found Sue's bag because her alarm clock went off. With that revelation, and the thought that the alarm probably startled the poor fellow to death, the four of us laughed and, in unison, said, "Liz!"

Heading back to the condo, we agreed that our stamina was waning. We were tired, and personally, my feet were killing me from my vain attempt at wearing cute shoes for the flight. At that point, all I wanted was a pair of soft tennis shoes. But, of course, they were sitting in Atlanta, waiting on the next flight. Trudging up the steps again, Dorothy whispered a little prayer as she inserted the key in the lock. Then, with a click, she opened the door to an absolutely stunning condo.

It held two bedrooms that were decorated in bright colors with several patterns of Mexican tiles in oranges and blues, and the beds were all in white with colorful runners across the foot of each one. The living room had a huge sectional sofa in various blues with several orange, red, and yellow throw pillows. There was a fully-equipped kitchen with vivid tile counter-tops and a dining area with comfortable leather chairs. The tabletop looked like a piece of art and had fruits of every kind painted around the edges. The colors of mangos, bananas, grapes, lemons, and oranges made us hungry just looking at them.

Dorothy had requested that the refrigerator be stocked in advance so we wouldn't need to find a restaurant the first evening, so together we made a huge salad. We sat on the balcony overlooking the sand and water as we took in the smells and sounds of the salt air and rolling seas. Listening to music, we couldn't help but mention how much Liz would have loved this time in Cabo. As hard as we tried to reminisce and regain our travel history of excitement and laughter, it just wouldn't come. Not that first night.

What Was That?

Katherine leaned over and hit me so hard I nearly fell out of my bed. I looked at the clock and saw it was just after four in the morning. She whispered, "I hear somebody at the door." I held my breath and listened. The front door creaked as it opened, and the two of us froze. My eyes rapidly searched our bedroom for any kind of weapon. Then we heard Dorothy thanking whomever it was at the front door for delivering our luggage. We heard her moving in the kitchen and soon smelled the fresh, satisfying aroma of coffee. Katherine and I could hear Dorothy whispering to Sue, and as thoughtful as that was, it was too late. The two of us were now wide awake; racing hearts make sleep less than possible.

We slipped on hotel robes and walked to the kitchen to join the pair. Sitting around the table sipping hot coffee and eating slices of fresh mango, we laughed over our near-death experience and discussed how exasperating it would be to put on our swimsuits. First of all, we all had snow-white skin, as it was still February in Atlanta. Secondly, winter alone brought on ten extra pounds minimum, with the holidays and Valentine's Day chocolates. The only silver lining was that I had taken time for a bright red pedicure; my feet would look marvelous. I only needed to figure out how to make them the focus of my anatomy rather than my spreading behind and thickening thighs.

Heading for the beach with hats, sunscreen, and cover-ups touching our ankles, we actually didn't feel too bad. Of course, the cute hats and makeup helped a great deal, and when we got to our assigned chairs and looked around at the competition, we decided aging vacationers were easy comparisons. Thank goodness it wasn't spring break.

Then the most exciting realization of the trip happened. We could lay right there on the lounge chairs and shop all day. They had different beach vendors who came along every ten minutes selling sterling silver jewelry, Mexican runners like the ones on our beds, Mexican rugs with colorful designs, and Chanel, Prada, and Gucci sunglasses for twenty dollars a pair. They were either the best buys in history or fakes, and we didn't care; they were cute. Then, when we thought it couldn't possibly get any better, vendors came with Fendi purses for twenty dollars. The surprise was that we bought nothing. Somehow, it just wasn't the same.

We didn't move from the lounge chairs for four hours, yet we were totally exhausted. Finally, it was time for Pina Coladas and afternoon snacks. As I took off my sunglasses, my eyes were drawn to my skin. It was now a bright red. We had enjoyed the beach for nearly five hours, and it was our first day in the hot Mexican sun. Who could remember to reapply sunscreen every hour when warm salty water was calling our names?

That night was miserable as we walked around like zombies trying to ensure nothing touched, including our inner thighs. This was after showers that nearly put us in the hospital from the intense pain. We decided to go into Cabo the next day for lunch and to try shopping, but all indoors. No sun.

Then we had another pleasant surprise. In Cabo, one doesn't need prescriptions for medications; everything is over the counter in the pharmacies. I never knew allopathic shopping was a possibility. We bought acne cream, cystitis and yeast infection medications, antibiotics, and anything we thought we might need in our aging lifetime. Obviously, we purchased every aloe product they had on their shelves. We loaded up our drugs and visited several jewelry stores and little beach boutiques. Yet, somehow, shopping had lost its flavor, so we had a late afternoon lunch and enjoyed delicious Mexican cuisine and strawberry margaritas.

That night we showered early and simply sat around in our nightgowns and allowed ourselves to talk about Liz. We relived so many of our adventures; one minute, we were howling with laughter, and the next, quiet with tears. But this time was important; we had given ourselves permission to hurt. It was a breakthrough for the four of us as we brought Liz back into every conversation from that point forward. The five of us were still together on so many levels.

The rest of that week consisted of more sun, albeit with plenty of sunscreen. However, it included one more trip to town so that we could purchase an additional suitcase. We had bought more medications then we had realized.

Is There Peace After Pain?

After our trip to Mexico, we were back to enjoying this close-knit friendship by having dinner at Houlihan's regularly and taking occasional trips to Sue's or Katherine's. But two years later, things began to change.

With the luxury of our retirement, Matt and I moved to our home on Bald Head Island permanently, though we kept the apartment in Atlanta. Then Sue retired and moved to her mountain house. Our dinners became fewer and further between. Our trips went from yearly to every two or three years at best. By now, Dorothy and Frank had retired and were living in Florida. However, Atlanta remained our central hub, and we met there any chance we could.

In Atlanta, we sometimes connected with Liz's girls, who handled their mother's death in their own manner. It hurt us to see their pain, but we felt it important for them to feel our love and share their memories. The four of us often met at the benches beside Liz's burial site to simply allow time to express our thoughts as we placed flowers. Strange how things are later in life. I think of others I have lost in this life and question if 'lost' is the best term. I think not.

I remember 'losing' my daddy. I never lost him. I can find him anytime through my memories and the love we shared. I remember "losing' my mother. She's not lost at all. I can still hear her calling my name, telling me to clean up my room, and assuring me that there is nothing I can't accomplish if I put my mind to it. Then I think about 'losing' Liz. She's as vivid to me today as the day she died. I can hear her laugh, see the twinkle in her eyes, and enjoy our talks through memories that can bring a smile each and every time. The friendship of the five of us is alive and well. Nothing is lost. And the five of us, plus Lilly, will one day be united in eternity.

As for me, and I'm sure it was true for all four of us, I would spend time after our visits in Atlanta remembering how blessed we were to have each other. The many years full of adventures that come along with the type of relationship the five of us shared. I hope I'm not giving the impression that I doubt this kind of friendship is available to all because I pray that every woman alive will enjoy such bonds. But as I reflect on our story of friendship, the devastation of cancer, and the difficulty of picking up the pieces, I realize the five of us and what we shared is more unusual than I first imagined. We just happened to be at the right place at the right time to form a bond that glued us together for a lifetime. A bond that left each of us crying out the words, "What I'd give for just one more anything."

A Continuation of the Introduction

(THE CONFESSION)

All of a sudden, a horn blared behind me. Startled, I glanced at my watch and realized I had been engrossed in a mixture of dreams and reminiscing for over three hours. Looking up to my rearview mirror, I saw Katherine, Dorothy, and Sue exiting their car. I got out of my car to meet them.

All at once, they started explaining various reasons for being late, including a misplaced purse and traffic on I-285. I waved off the excuses and began giving hugs. Together we trudged the long muddy climb to the bell tower. Upon reaching the top, we stomped as much mud off our shoes as possible, then walked over to Liz's grave site. We said a prayer and watched Katherine place a dozen red roses in the vase at the top of the marble headstone. Then, we quietly took our usual places on the benches we had occupied so many times before.

After a moment, Katherine huffed, "Jan, are you okay? Why this urgent meeting?"

I nodded and said, "I'm fine."

Showing relief, she laughed and mused, "Have we gotten a multimillion-dollar offer on our *Mount Rundel* painting?"

I laughed and replied, "No, I'm afraid not."

Dorothy then fussed, "You've scared us to death! What's the matter?"

I gave a half-smile along with a mischievous grin as I reached into my rather large purse. Pulling out three rectangular items wrapped in tissue paper, I confessed, "Ladies, our story has been immortalized!" Then, I shrugged, "I've written a book!"

Book Club Discussion Questions

1. Does this book remind you of some of your friends? A group of friends whom you enjoy?
2. How did your group form? Did any common denominators or shared interests contribute?
3. Has your group suffered a tragedy or heartbreak?
4. How did you face the difficult times, and what helped bring your group through those hardships?
5. Are there times when your friendship gets in the way of other relationships?
6. What is the most significant challenge your group faces at the present time?

7. What are your concerns about remaining close as you grow older, and as your lives take different directions?
8. Have you and your group ever discussed the prospect of heaven?
9. Does your group ever pray together to show your support and hope for one another?
10. Share a few favorite memories of times together with your group.

Books on Heaven

A Case for Heaven by Lee Strobel

A Divine Revelation of Heaven by Mary K. Baxter

Heaven by Randy Alcorn

Heaven is for Real by Todd Burpo

Miracles from Heaven by Christy Wilson Beam

The Heaven Answer Book by Billy Graham

Any Bible Concordance—simply look up the word 'heaven' and you will find several helpful scriptures that will introduce you to the topic of eternity.

More from J Boykin Baker

The By Design Trilogy
An emotional and sweet romance that is guaranteed to touch the heart of anyone who has experienced the breathtaking intensity of a new love.

Paperbacks, ebooks and audiobook are available on Amazon.

Books are also available in bookstores.

Author Contact:
JBoykinBaker.com

By Design, Book 1

SNEAK PEEK

Introduction

Gretchen Boyd had a wonderful life. She was blessed with a successful and loving husband, a sweet and beautiful teenage daughter, supportive family and friends, but most importantly, she had her faith which she was counting on to serve her well. Gretchen was fun-loving and adventurous in such creative ways. She had always embraced life to its fullest. But now she was sick and her life was changing.

A virulent form of cancer was invading her body and, barring a miracle, it would most likely take her life. It was a devastating diagnosis for herself, but her worst fears were for her only child, Anne. How would her precious fourteen-year-old daughter navigate her future, all of life's decisions, without a mother to guide her? Sadness flooded her thoughts as she visualized each of the special moments in Anne's future that she would probably miss. Choking up, she imagined graduation, her prom, her first boyfriend, her first job . . . her wedding. These thoughts were way too painful; she shifted her attention to her husband.

Edward was a good daddy and he was crazy about Anne, but his work was demanding. There were nights before a court case that he didn't get home until close to midnight. Who would be there for Anne to help her with schoolwork and take her to activities? Who would hold her as she poured her heart out when she'd had a bad day? Who would be there to keep her from being lonely and sad when she'd walk into an empty house?

Gretchen looked at her watch. It was time for her medicine. The pain seemed to be increasing daily, and she needed to get it under control before Anne came rushing in from play practice. She swallowed the capsule with a drink of iced tea. Stepping out of her shoes, she pulled the covers back on her bed and lay down, trying to get comfortable as she winced and waited for the pill to do its job. The thought of her situation was now all too real. Tears flooded her eyes as she began to make a mental list of her family's future needs.

By the end of the next week, Gretchen had hired Ruby Wheeler, a jovial, kind and experienced housekeeper who could work full-time and even stay late when necessary.

Ruby had known Anne since she was five from the years she had worked as part nanny, part housekeeper for one of Edward's cousins. She was to start in two weeks so that Anne and Edward could get accustomed to her, and Ruby could get familiar with their lifestyle and schedules.

Next, Gretchen insisted Edward take a day off. She needed to discuss his responsibilities concerning their daughter, things he would not naturally think to do. Through their tears she had gotten a solemn promise that he understood and would always put their daughter's needs above everything.

Then, she interviewed Ruth Kelly, a well-respected grief counselor. After several hours of discussing her medical situation and concerns for Anne and her husband, Gretchen was comfortable with her choice. That night Gretchen gently presented Ruth's card to Edward. She gave him a kiss and told him to put the card where he could easily find it when the time came. Edward looked at the card, back at his wife and took her in his arms. Not another word was said.

The days passed, and as Gretchen's condition grew worse, all she could think about were the decisions that Anne might face. One afternoon she walked to the back door, turned to a board with old painted hooks, and reached for her tan sweater. She smiled, remembering knitting that sweater when she was expecting Anne. It seemed such a short time ago, but Anne was already a budding teenager. Continuing to the porch, she sat down in a rocking chair. It was a startlingly clear autumn day, blue skies overhead, and the leaves were starting to change. The kind of day that makes you want to live forever, but then, no one does. Gretchen held her hands up and turned them slowly; how frail and helpless she felt at just forty years of age. In the last few weeks, she could actually feel herself slipping away. She began to pray.

"Dear God, please give me wisdom and clarity for a plan that will honor you and help my sweet girl in times to come. I know you'll be with her, Lord, and that is such comfort, but please help me leave a legacy that will stand in my stead."

While she prayed, her mind began to fill with ideas for guiding Anne on her journey to womanhood.

As she reviewed her thoughts, Gretchen was clear that the design for this plan had to fit any needs or questions that might arise, and it had to equip her daughter to make wise choices concerning subjects as broad as friends, finances, college, and eventually the possibility of marriage. The plan had to be profound, yet simple, so that Anne could recall its steps at a moment's notice. Gretchen searched her memory for past situations the two had tackled. One immediately came to mind.

. . .

Years earlier, Gretchen had watched Anne struggle with her allowance, usually coming up short with days to go. She smiled as she remembered the distress her daughter experienced when she had no money left for a movie with her friends. One afternoon when Anne was throwing a tantrum over this very subject and was begging for an advance "just this one last time," mother and daughter sat down on the bed in Anne's room. With some thought, even an argument or two, they developed a system they named the "Three S's," a plan to assist in controlling Anne's spending and temper when things didn't go her way.

Going forward, Anne would divide her allowance into three jars. She could wisely spend the eighty percent in the first jar, save ten percent for emergencies in the second, and still have ten percent remaining in the third to share with children in need or church projects. It took a little time for Anne to get the system down pat, but in the end, a more successful money management process developed. Gretchen nodded as her thoughts began to give birth to a new three-step plan, but this plan would be a guide for Anne's life journey.

She opened the small drawer to her nightstand and picked up a bright floral journal, a treasured Mother's Day gift from Anne. She opened the book to the inscription on the first page: "To the most wonderful mother in the whole wide world, I love you sooo much!!!" Tears filled her eyes. She took a tissue out of her pocket and sat down at Edward's desk. She picked up a pen, turned to a fresh page, dabbed her eyes, and began to write.

A design for the new plan seemed to flow. The first step of the plan would start with Anne identifying her desire or concern regarding a specific issue. With the issue identified, whether it was friends, money, career-direction, or more, the second step would be an evaluation of possible choices or decisions. In the third step, Anne would need to consider how her selected choice would affect the outcome of her intended goal or destiny.

Gretchen knew this three-step plan was not as simple as it sounded. There would likely be struggles and heartbreak along the way, as some choices could be painful. But that pain would be nothing compared to the consequences of Anne being untrue to what she knew was right in her heart. Ignoring her conscience and making compromises could prevent attaining her goal or realizing her greatest destiny.

Feeling tired, Gretchen moved to her bed. Removing her shoes, she tugged at a small woolen throw to lay it over her feet and settled back against the comfort of her pillows. It was time to mentally test her plan. Gretchen smiled as a thought began to materialize. She could use an imaginary scenario concerning friendship. Suppose Anne was introduced to a new friend, but soon found this friend was using cheat sheets on algebra tests. Not only that, her friend would ask to copy Anne's homework. Would Anne value the friendship so much that she would take a chance of her friend's bad habits getting her in trouble? Or would she make the difficult choice to kindly discontinue the friendship and avoid possibly being labeled as dishonest? A label like that could undermine the trust of her teachers, cause suspicion regarding test scores, possibly limit college choices due to lukewarm recommendations, and jeopardize her long-standing desire of becoming an interior designer. Gretchen smiled. *It works!* Her plan was complete. It all basically came down to three questions.

First, what desire or concern came into play?

Second, what choice and commitment were required to stay true to herself?

Third, how could that choice and commitment affect her goal or destiny?

All was ready to begin discussions with her daughter.

About a week later, Ruby had a church meeting, Edward was going to be working late, and the perfect opportunity presented itself. Journal in hand, Gretchen called Anne into her bedroom and patted for her to come snuggle and chat for a little while. It was their normal custom in the late afternoon before dinner and homework. They settled in as Gretchen shared the "new friend scenario." She felt it was a good way to illustrate her train of thought as she introduced her plan.

"Now, let's talk about money. What is your future desire concerning your finances, sweetheart?"

Anne turned over and rested her face in her hands as she thought and finally said, "Money is not a big deal to me. I would just like to have a lot, and I don't want to give out. And remember, I want to give some to help children."

Gretchen smiled, "So what kind of choice would it take for you not to give out and to be able to help?"

"Other than asking Daddy if I could have one of his credit cards?" Anne said with a laugh. "I guess a choice to get a job and not spend more than I'm paid." She laid back and put her head in her mother's lap.

"And how would a job and living on a budget affect your destiny?" Gretchen continued as she stroked her daughter's hair.

Anne's eyes lit up. "I would always have enough to do the 'Three S's.' I could help children with the sharing part."

Both smiled as they thought of that earlier lesson. Mother and daughter continued to examine various choices and consequences with school work, activities, colleges, and more.

Yet Gretchen had designed her plan to include an

even more serious conversation. She took a breath. "Now, let's talk about boys."

"M-o-t-h-e-r, I really don't have that desire. I hope you're not going to talk about sex stuff . . . that's gross." A flushed rosy glow began at Anne's neck and spread to her cheeks.

Gretchen smiled at her daughter's familiar blush. "But you will have that desire. It may not be important to you now, but take my word, sooner than you know it's going to become important. You will be very attractive to the young men you meet."

"Mother, can we get a glass of tea, I need a snack or something?"

Anne wasn't thirsty or hungry, but she was beginning to understand her mother's purpose for the plan and her eyes filled with tears. She wiped her face as tears spilled and angrily turned to her mother. "I don't want to learn all of this stuff. I want you to be here to help me. I don't want to grow up without you!"

Gretchen took Anne's hand. "I know."

She tenderly wrapped her arms around her daughter. Anne settled back against the soft pillows and the two snuggled in silence until there were no more tears.

Gretchen gently restarted the conversation and whispered, "We'll have a glass of tea a little later. Let's think this through."

She knew the discussion was difficult for Anne and took it slowly, but she needed to persist. "Suppose you're out with a young man and he starts making sexual advances that seem rather exciting . . . you'll have a choice to make. Will you want a trial run or will you save that part of yourself for the man you marry? The choice to wait will require a serious commitment and trust me, it will not be easy. Making love is a beautiful part of a committed relationship, but can have painful consequences outside of marriage. Painful breakups, health issues, unplanned pregnancies, and sadly, even the pressure of an abortion. The choice not to wait could seriously affect your destiny."

"Mother, all of this seems a million years away."

Still as they talked, Anne could tell how important their conversation was to her mother and reluctantly decided to listen as she rubbed the back of her mother's hand on her cheek.

"It does right now, sweetheart, but you'll need to be committed to your choice before you face a crisis in the heat of the moment. I pray that you will carefully think through how your decision could affect your life. Always remember, sweetheart, make your decisions knowing that your worth is invaluable."

Gretchen fluffed her pillows and sat up a little straighter. "Let me tell you a couple of stories to help you better understand. One of my friends had a strong desire to care for children. She and her husband had two biological children and adopted three others. Several years later, she learned of three young sisters who desperately needed a home. She was faced with two choices. Would she raise her existing family just as it was, or would she adopt the young girls, and nurture them as well? Not an easy decision. How would the addition of three more children affect her home and family life? After much thought and prayer, she made the choice to follow her heart and adopted the sisters. Today, because of that heartfelt choice, her destiny has mushroomed into a ministry for orphans. That one unselfish choice has improved the lives of thousands of children."

"Now, let me tell you about another friend who because of insecurities had a basic desire to ensure the happiness of others, even at the expense of her own. Because she wanted to please, she chose to give in to a young man's fleeting satisfaction, and with that choice, her life evolved into an unwanted pregnancy and a desperate abortion. Deserted by both the father and her parents, and filled with guilt, that unfortunate choice directed her life down a sad and negative path. Thankfully, with prayer, she was able to forgive herself, and even wrote a book, *Heavenly Appointments*. A sweet story aimed at helping other young women come to terms with guilt and embrace forgiveness. Even though it took time, better choices have her back on track for a more positive destiny with a wonderful husband and three beautiful children."

Gretchen looked intently into her daughter's eyes. "Anne, as hard as you try to make the very best choices, there may be times when you will make a mistake. Just remember, you can go back to the plan by making better choices. You have the power to choose again, follow your heart, and move your destiny in a better direction."

Gretchen paused. "But my sweet girl, even with God's grace, because of His love for us, there are consequences when we're disobedient and don't follow our hearts. Those consequences can cause a delay or disruption in His best plan for us. My prayer for you, my sweet girl, is that your goals and desires will be so meaningful that you will seek strength and wisdom to make the best choices. And that those choices will allow God to give you the desires of your heart as He reveals His perfect destiny for your precious life."

Thirteen years later . . .

Anne smiled through tears as she reflected on her mother's careful design for her future, and for the most part the plan had worked beautifully. Sure, she had made the typical mistakes, but nothing serious. It only took once to realize that bouncing a check, confiding in a gossip, or drinking more than two beers were bad ideas. So . . . nothing major.

In fact, the plan had been working for all the important choices in her life until Anne gazed into the dark brown eyes of Bradford Young.

By Design, Book 1

SNEAK PEEK

Chapter One

"Well, hello there. What can I do for you, young lady?" Such a simple greeting, but it had taken Anne Boyd's breath away as she stared into the deepest brown eyes she had ever seen.

Thinking back to that first meeting with Dr. Bradford Young, Jr., she laughed as she remembered how those engaging eyes had checked her out in a most obvious manner, and how their time together hadn't seemed like a first meeting at all. In fact, it was as if she had known him, or at least the dream of him, forever.

She sighed as she snuggled into her chair, laid her head back, and thought; *everything is happening so fast.* In what seemed like an instant, her life had been turned upside down, but the upheaval she was experiencing was thrilling. Each event . . . each change . . . brought new and exciting experiences, even down to the street noises that first morning as she had searched for a hazelnut latte. She closed her eyes and began to drift back to the chaotic, yet appealing sounds of this wide-awake Southern metropolis.

Anne listened to horns blaring and brakes squealing as cars jostled to switch lanes on Peachtree Street. Atlanta was quite a change from the slower pace of Richmond. Not a bad change, just a different, much more energetic change. She could even sense a burst of exhilaration in the warm spring air while it whirled all around. As she watched the effects of the breezes swirling higher and higher, she lifted her eyes.

Glancing up, Anne smiled. Centered in an expanse of blue was a single white puffy cloud. It had to be a good sign. She had always loved the fairytale qualities of billowy clouds ever since she was a little girl sprawled on top of the rickety grey picnic table in her backyard. She loved to lie there and imagine the clouds as puffs of freshly spun sugar. You know, like the layers of pastel softness that swallow those puny little paper cones—cotton candy that makes your mouth water when the aroma fills the air at any North Carolina beach. Imagining that sweet, melting sensation, she had to admit this was starting out to be a great day. Not only had she spotted that plump little cloud, she had also found an empty parking space on Peachtree. Two miracles and it wasn't even seven o'clock! Anne cautiously opened her car door, slipped out, and began her quest for supposedly the best latte in the city.

Looking around, she was amazed that the business district was bustling with so many pedestrians this early. She turned and slowly began to follow the crowd. Checking her directions, she figured some of these folks were bound to be headed to Mugs, the famous coffee shop she had heard so much about. Anyway, Anne wasn't in a hurry and just felt like taking her time as she enjoyed her stroll through a maze of concrete, flowering trees, and bright green patches of grass.

She couldn't have ordered a more beautiful day if she'd tried. But then, what more could she have expected? Spring was a delightful season in Atlanta. There were profusions of azaleas, daffodils, and dogwoods that seemed to dot every lawn, assuring a most colorful time of year in the South. She leaned down to take in the fragrance of the different petals, but suddenly felt compelled to stand and just listen. She could hear a slight rustling of the trees. Just then, the sound seemed to get louder as if magically amplified above the street noise. She could feel the lightest air weaving through her long brown hair and was convinced the enchanted breeze was whispering, "Welcome to Atlanta, Anne Boyd." Turning her face, she felt a subtle gust brush her cheek as if to complete the greeting by depositing a playful kiss.

She sighed and checked her watch; there was no more time for daydreaming. She refocused and continued her mission to find the old café which, according to friends, served the best gourmet coffees in town.

Now, walking a little faster, she smiled. A distinct coffee aroma was filling the air. She stepped over to the left and peered as far down the sidewalk as possible, but there was still no café in sight. Then, out of the corner of her eye, she saw a man exit a door with a tall paper cup in his hand. Growing closer, she was stunned to find the most unexpected little fifties diner nestled in the middle of mammoth, gleaming skyscrapers. In the window a yellow neon sign blinked out "MUGS, Atlanta's Best Coffees."

Entering the shiny, rounded building, she took her place in the long line. She glanced around at the crowded space, smiling at different people as their eyes met. She was a little surprised to find the counter and floor a bit messy in comparison to the popular coffee shops back in Richmond, but then again, those shops were not nearly this busy. Besides, she was enjoying this new experience too much to care. As she watched the line grow longer and longer, she realized nearly everyone else in the city apparently had converged to begin their day with a jolt of caffeine.

"One large skinny latte please, with a shot of

hazelnut." She shrugged and added, "And lots of sugar."

The barista grinned as he filled her order and handed her the steaming cup. Glancing over, she watched a man fold his paper to possibly leave. As he stood, she smiled and slid into his empty stool. She couldn't wait to enjoy the taste and smell of the infamous latte that was finally in her hand. She took a sip; it tasted smooth and delicious. She propped her elbows on the counter and savored the cup as she imagined the exciting day that lay ahead.

Anne was still finding it hard to believe she was actually living in Atlanta and was beginning her new job with one of the largest design firms in the South. "Beginning her new job," those words seemed to echo as she thought back over the last eight years.

Having graduated from Virginia Commonwealth University four years earlier, she had landed a one-year internship with S. Herndon Architects, and was then hired by Catherine Turpin, Richmond's best-known hotel and resort designer. Anne had loved that job, but after three years of constant traveling to project locations, she was getting restless and was ready for a change and new challenges. A bigger city like Atlanta promised both. One evening while searching online, her eye caught an opening for a senior design position at the high-end commercial design firm, Wilson Interiors. The firm had one opening. Anne sent her resume, received a call, flew to Atlanta, interviewed, and got the job.

On the plane back to Richmond, she pulled out a worn floral journal. Rubbing her hand over the faded handwriting of her mother's plan, her eyes followed the three steps. Her passion was definitely interior design. She was making the brave choice to change locations and leave friends to advance her career. Now, just a few weeks later, she was beginning her new job in a thriving city. The next step to her destiny had been set into motion.

Anne's eyes moistened as she thought of her mother's adventurous personality and how supportive she'd be about this new opportunity. With that tender thought, a caffeine rush and sheer exhilaration, she was ready for her new life to begin! Anne finished the last sip, tossed her cup, stretched and smiled , "Wilson Interiors—here I come!" Then she panicked as she hurried to retrace her steps. She had no idea where she had parked.

Following a successful search, Anne pulled up to her new workplace and drove slowly into the parking lot. She was still awed by the sight of the stark white building which would now become her new workday home. She parked, then began to examine the two distinct features of this unique landmark, known as the Wilson Building. The architecture was definitely contemporary and reflected Atlanta's more modern business district. However, the ultra-modern structures of the district seemed an oddity in this historically Southern city which was steeped in traditional English roots. As she admired the building, she glanced through a small clearing as the bright morning glare began to soften. She could see inside. The huge glass panels were revealing an interior view. The lobby was stunning white marble with classic furnishings. The trim was traditional to its core, including fluted columns and scrolling pediments. There were colorful Persian rugs, bronze and crystal lighting, and lots of English antiques. It was as if two worlds had come together to form one double-minded structure. She smiled. *Art imitating life . . . old struggling to remain new and new struggling to replace the old.*

Gathering her books, briefcase, and purse, Anne approached the building. She was more than excited and assured herself that she was prepared. Knowing this opportunity was a big chance, she was ready to walk through that door and begin the next phase of her career. Then she laughed as she thought back to her strange interview. She had not necessarily been hired because of her brilliance or talent. To Anne's amazement, she knew deep down that she had actually been hired because of her eyes. Juggling books and belongings, she struggled to pull the thick glass door open as she thought back to the morning of her interview. She had been nothing but a bundle of nerves.

. . .

The reception room had been filled with nine possible candidates that day, all of whom were vying for the only opening Wilson had offered in three years. Anne handed her resume to the receptionist, settled into a pretty, but uncomfortable, blue chair, and began to canvas the room. The decor was impressive. It reminded Anne of her trip to London and some of the elegant English drawing rooms she had visited. The room was beautiful with its gold leaf, handsome oil paintings, and period furnishings—all of which seemed so striking against the bright white backdrop of formal English architecture. *Very nice!* Anne settled in for what she expected to be a long wait. She checked her cell.

Just then a well-dressed man sporting a plaid French beret rushed through the entrance. He slowed down and began to look around, then nodded, crossed the room and entered a private door. In a few minutes, he opened the door to an adjoining room and peeked out. He was looking directly at Anne.

What is he looking at? She checked her skirt and looked up just in time to see him peek out again. Then he opened the door.

"You in the blue chair . . . what's your name?" the man asked.

Anne glanced down to reassure herself the chair was still blue and answered, "Anne Boyd."

"Well, Miss Boyd, come on back."

She entered the door and followed him down a wide corridor wondering how she was fortunate enough to be the first interviewee. They entered a huge paneled conference room through double doors. The first thing she noticed were two bronze chandeliers perfectly spaced over an inlaid mahogany conference table. The walls were filled with bookcases bulging with colorful old leather books, and at least two dozen brown, leather chairs surrounded the table, all of which displayed an ornate "WI" engraved in bronze on the backs. She could hardly breathe as she took in the most intimidating setting imaginable for a job interview. As she stood there, feeling every nerve in her body, she prayed she would not faint or throw up.

Ben Wilson, president of Wilson Interiors, took a seat at the far end of the table, removed his beret, tossed it artfully into a bowl that was centered on the table, smiled triumphantly, then motioned for her to come closer as he pointed to a chair.

"Tell me about yourself, Miss Boyd, and let's take a look at your portfolio."

Anne froze! Having been so flustered when he called her back, she had forgotten to pick up her portfolio case. It was still sitting by the blue chair in the waiting room. Knowing this blunder could lead to a less than favorable first impression, she had to think fast.

With all the courage she could muster, she blurted out, "Mr. Wilson, before I present my portfolio, I'd love to have a conversation with you about how I feel my design skills and experience can hopefully be an asset to your firm. That will give you something to mull over while I run back to the reception room to grab my portfolio." She gave him a shrug and a questioning smile.

Mr. Wilson grinned. "No problem." Then he yelled at the top of his voice, "Martha, please get Miss Boyd's portfolio case. It's probably by that blue chair in the reception room."

He chuckled to himself as he continued to review her resume. "It happens all the time."

Moments later, Martha rushed in with the case and handed it to Anne. She and Mr. Wilson spent about thirty minutes covering each project represented, along with a few of the corresponding details.

Then he said the strangest thing. "Anne, I want to apologize for staring at you this morning, but I lost my younger sister, Claire, about four years ago and I miss her. When I saw you . . . well, I saw her brown eyes again, even that softness that could melt my heart."

Anne did have the softest brown eyes, and they could tear up at the drop of a hat when she was moved by beauty or sadness, and when watching old movies, a favorite pastime. She felt sorry for Mr. Wilson and was grateful that her eyes had helped to strengthen his memories, but she was embarrassed when she felt tears beginning to form.

"I'm sorry about your sister." She lowered her head to wipe her eyes. "I understand how difficult it is to lose someone you love, especially when it's way too soon."

Mr. Wilson looked at Anne, then yelled to Martha, "The interviews are over. Send everyone home." He turned to Anne with a smile and said, "The eyes have it."

Anne thanked him and silently thanked her parents for her eyes.

"Study up on corporate and medical rules and regulations, Miss Boyd. We'll start you on a few of those projects. Learn accessibility, building, and all related codes. Be ready."

Mr. Wilson excused himself and walked out. He yelled down the hall as he disappeared, "Martha, give Anne copies of all the Wilson how's and why's and get her started on employee paperwork."

That interview had been a month ago and now there was not a code in the state of Georgia that Anne had not committed to memory. She walked into the building, entered the Wilson Interiors suite, and stopped at Martha's desk.

"Anne Boyd reporting for duty," she said with what she hoped would appear to be confident smile.

Martha welcomed her and guided Anne from office to office as she introduced Wilson's newest employee to the other ten designers. Each one was busy as they thumbed through fabrics, took calls or tackled paperwork. She could tell there would be little time for socializing. Then Martha ushered Anne into her new, very neutral office. There were two black project folders already open on her desk. She sat down and couldn't wait to get started. After reading every word in both folders, she sat back in her very own brown, leather chair, spun around, and exhaled. She could only imagine the adventures that lay ahead!

About the Author

 J Boykin Baker grew up in the small town of Wilson, North Carolina. She knew from the age of seven, after seeing the old movie "Pillow Talke," that the only career for her was interior design. After college, marriage, and babies, her dream of being an interior designer came true with the start of her own design firm in Atlanta, Georgia. As luck would have it, she just happened to be in the right place—at the right time—with the right look and ended up designing hospitals, corporate offices, and high-end residential projects nationwide.During her years as President of Baker Interiors, Inc., she had the privilege of working with countless women. Due to her caring nature, she was led to mentor young women through familiar struggles of a reoccurring nature. Eventually, she carried her love for women and children even further when she founded a non-profit, Widow's Mite Experience, Inc., to provide emergency water relief for families in the United States and around the world. With the help of

hundreds of women volunteers, the ministry is now active in 32 countries and/or provinces.

Her writing career began with a series of children's books illustrating the unusual travels of a doll named Mary Margaret. She has written two pilots that explore the lives of Southern women, and has had various interiors and commentaries published in national magazines. Under duress, she has even written two professional manuals. She recently completed the *By Design* trilogy covering the joys, challenges, and struggles of a woman's life, from the intensity of new love through the pressures of balancing family and career, and finally, to the point of leaving a legacy for future generations.

With humor, tears, and professional insight, this bestselling author enjoys sharing her wide-ranging experiences in her writings, on national television, in radio interviews, and speaking to international audiences. She was named one of North Carolina's Women of Achievement and was a winner of the 2023 International Impact Book Award for her *By Design* trilogy. In a nutshell, J Boykin Baker continues to thoroughly enjoy a full and adventurous life!

~

Thank you for purchasing *One More Anything*. By doing so, you are helping to send clean water to flood-ravaged areas in the United States and disparate water-deprived countries abroad. Fifty percent of all author profits from this book will be donated to the Christian Broadcasting Network (CBN), a 501(c)(3) non-profit ministry.

https://www.cbn.org

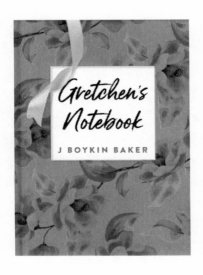

~

Dear Treasured Reader

Please send me your email and I will be delighted to email you a gift copy of Gretchen's Notebook. There are pages reserved in the back for you to write down cherished thoughts and a beautiful plan to help lovingly direct those you love! Gretchen's plan for her daughter is the Introduction to your Sneak Peek of By Design, Book One. Hope it gives you some wonderful ideas for your very own notebook! Look forward to hearing from you!

Blessings!
JBoykinBaker.com

Made in United States
North Haven, CT
21 July 2023

39371805R00148